W9-AZF-038

Kwame: An American Hero

Written by

Richard Jeanty

RJ Publications, LLC

Newark, New Jersey

RJ Publications
richjeanty@yahoo.com
www.rjpublications.com
Copyright © 2012 by Richard Jeanty
All Rights Reserved
ISBN-10: 0981999875

ISBN-13: 978-0981999876

Printed in the United States

February 2012

1 2 3 4 5 6 7 8 9 10

Acknowledgements

First, I would like to thank my daughter, Rishanna Jeanty, for coming into my life. You have been my muse for the last six years. I love you with all my heart. I want to thank Chanel Caraway for her great assistance with the editing and proofreading of this book. I appreciate you with all my heart. I want to thank all the special people in my life; Delores, my father, my mother, my siblings, nephews and nieces, and all those people who have supported me from the very beginning. All of you play a specific role in my life.

Special thanks go out to my main man, Christopher Bell, aka Chris B, The Bookman in Brooklyn, for all your assistance with this book. Your guidance in helping me identify the right trains, streets, train station, and other areas in Brownsville that I would not have known, is appreciated. Your knowledge of Brooklyn cut my research down tremendously. I'm glad I didn't have to drive all over Brooklyn to learn some of these areas. I also want to thank you for pushing all the RJ Publications titles on your stands around New York.

I also would like to thank Pogo and Ali in the Bronx, Max in Brooklyn, Akeion in Brooklyn, Grace and Harris in Brooklyn, Henry in Harlem and all the book vendors, distributors and bookstores that make it possible for my books to reach the readers.

Last but not least, I want to send out a big thank you to Frugal Books in Boston for always showing me the best hometown love.

Introduction

Ever since the election of President Obama, most Black Americans have felt they have finally found their hero. Mr. Obama is indeed a hero in many ways to many of us because of his accomplishment as the first elected Black president in these United States. We'll forever be indebted to him for reassuring the world that we are bright and capable and opening the highest door that we could've ever possibly thought was available to us. However, I have a question: if you had a chance to become a real hero to the people in your own community, what would you do?

Too many of us walk around the hood without a care for our fellow man. Often times, we turn a blind eye to the struggle, the financial pain, the physical pain, the emotional pain, the lack of education, the hunger, the mental instability, the physical incapabilities, and the overall well-being of our fellow man.

In the fifties and sixties, we had leaders who were willing to sacrifice their own lives for the betterment of our community. Those people were the leaders who opened the doors for the modern day rappers, singers, boxers, football players, basketball players, writers, doctors, president, CEO's and pilots. Was their sacrifice in vain? What have we contributed to their movement in this new century and era? Better yet, who's going to be the new leader of tomorrow, you? Have we lost the true meaning of leadership? Dr. Martin Luther King, Malcolm X, Frederick Douglas, Arthur Ashe, W.E.B. Dubois and many other leaders and activists who came before us are probably turning over in their graves while watching what we have become as a community.

I wanted to write a book about a hero, but a different hero, one who loves his family, cares about his community and is willing to sacrifice his own life for the sake of others. Well, I hope I was able to accomplish the said mission with Kwame. Everybody needs a hero for encouragement, so please make sure all your heroic efforts start at home and in your community. We have plenty of young minds being molded and influenced by the heroes they see everyday, good or bad.

The streets are calling

Kwame's war against the most ruthless drug gang in Brownsville, led up to his one-man attack of the hardest penetrated fortress there ever was in the hood. If he could penetrate that fortress so easily by himself, he wondered how the cops could act like it didn't exist. The two men standing guard at the door didn't even see him coming. The loud thump of a punch to the throat of the 6ft-5-inch giant guarding the door with his life, had the breath taken right out of him with that one punch. He stumbled to the ground without any hope of ever getting back up. His partner noticed the swift and effective delivery of the man's punch, and thought twice about approaching him. Running would be the smartest option at this time, but how cowardice that would be? The attacker was but five feet ten inches tall and perhaps one hundred and ninety pounds in weight. The security guard didn't have time on his side and before he could contemplate his next move, the masked attacker wearing army fatigues, unloaded a kick to his groin that sent his 6ft-7inch frame bowing in pain while holding his nuts for soothing comfort. Another blow to the temple followed, and the man was out permanently.

At first glance, Kwame didn't stand a chance against the two giants guarding the front door. One weighed just a little less than three hundred and twenty five pounds, and the other looked like an NFL lineman at three hundred and sixty pounds. However, Kwame was a trained Navy SEAL. He came home to find that the people closest to him were embroiled in a battle that threatened their livelihood daily. His sister, Jackie, became a crackhead while his mother, Janice, was a heroin addict. Two different types of drugs in one household, under the same roof, were enough to drive him crazy. Kwame didn't even recognize his sister, at first. She had aged at least twice her real age and his mother was completely unrecognizable. He left her a strong woman when he joined the Navy six years prior, but he came back to find his whole family had been under the control of drug dealers and the influence of drugs, and Kwame set out to do something about it.

The two giants at the door was just the beginning of his battle to get to the high level dealers who controlled the streets where he grew up. As he made his way down the long dark corridor, he could see women with their breasts bare and fully naked, bagging the supplies of drugs for distribution throughout the community. Swift on his feet like a fast moving kitten, Kwame was unnoticeable. He could hear the loud voices of men talking about their plans to rack up another million dollars from the neighborhood through their drug distribution by week's end. The strong smell of ganja clouded the air as he approached the doorway to meet his nemesis. Without saying a word after setting foot in the room, he shot the first man who took notice of him right in the head. Outnumbered six-to-one, magazine clips sitting on the tables by the dozen, and loaded weapons at the reach of every person in the room, Kwame had to act fast. It was a brief standoff before the first guy reached for his 9Millimeter automatic weapon, and just like that, he found himself engulfed in a battle with flying bullets from his chest all the way down to his toes. Pandemonium broke and everybody reached for their guns at once. As Kwame rolled around on his back on the floor with a .44 Magnum in each hand, all five men were shot once in the head and each fell dead to the floor before they had a chance to discharge their weapons. The naked women ran for their lives as the barrage of gunshots sent them into a frenzy. The masked gun man dressed in Army fatigues was irrelevant to them. It was time to get the hell out of dodge to a safe place, away from the stash house. Not worried too much about the innocent women, Kwame pulled out a laundry bag and started filling it up with the stacks of money on the table. By the time he was done, he had estimated at least a couple of million dollars was confiscated for the good of the community. The back door was the quickest and safest exit without being noticed. After throwing the bag of money over a wall separating the stash house from the next house, Kwame lit his match and threw it on the gasoline track that he had poured before entering the house. The house was set ablaze and no evidence was left behind for the cops to build a case. It was one of the worst fires that Brownsville had seen in many years. No traces of human bones were left, as everything burned down to ashes by the time the New York Fire Department responded.

Kwame had been watching the house for weeks and he intended on getting rid of everything, including the people behind the big drug operation that was destroying his community. Before going to the front of the house to get rid of the security guards, he had laid out his plan to burn down the house if he couldn't get past them. A gallon of gasoline was poured in front of all the doors, except the front way where the two bouncers stood guard. His plan was to start the fire in the back and quickly rush to the front to pour out more gasoline to block every possible exit way, but that was his last option. His first option was to grab some of the money to begin his plans to finance the local community center for the neighborhood kids. His first option worked and it was on to the next house.

When Kwame came home to find his mother and sister almost a shell of what he left behind, he was determined to get rid of the bad elements in his neighborhood. Mad that he had to leave home to escape the belly of the beast, Kwame came back with a vengeance. He wanted to give every little boy and little girl in his neighborhood a chance at survival and a future. He understood that the military did him some good, but he had to work twice as hard to even get considered for the elite Navy SEALs. The military was something that he definitely didn't want any boys from his neighborhood to join. For him, it was his best option and in the end, he made the most of it. Guerilla warfare was the most precious lesson he learned while in the military, and it was those tactics that he'd planned on using to clean up his neighborhood. Kwame wanted to do it all alone. A one man show meant that only he could be the cause of his own demise. There'd be no snitches to worry about, no outside help, no betrayal and most of all, no deception from anybody. Self- reliance was one of the training tactics he also learned in the Navy and it was time for him to apply all that he learned to make his community all it could be.

Getting rid of that stash house was one of his first missions. Kwame had seen the crack houses sprouting all over the neighborhood and it would take precise planning on his part to get rid of them one by one, without getting caught by the police. Kwame also knew that he wasn't just going to be fighting the drug dealers, but some of the crooked cops that were part of the criminal enterprise plaguing the hood as well. At this point, Kwame was one up on the "Benjamins Click," one of the most dangerous drug gangs in Brownsville, Brooklyn. It was just the beginning of a long fight, but the history behind what led to this point is the most fascinating aspect of Kwame's story.

The Father

Jack and Janice Robinson had just graduated from high school when Janice became pregnant with their first child, Kwame. Marriage was automatic as Jack and Janice were in love, and Jack was a stand-up guy who wanted to make sure they were a family. People even referred to the couple affectionately as "Double J" whenever they were together, and due to the fact their names were Jack and Janice. It was 1987 when Jack made the decision to join the United States Marines so he could provide financially for his family. Janice was the happiest woman after Jack proposed to her and a small wedding soon followed. Since neither of them came from wealthy families, both sides had to chip in so that the wedding could take place. Janice was a beautiful pregnant bride. Her stomach hardly showed because she was still in her first trimester. She was happy to marry Jack, her first love. Both sides of the family welcomed baby Kwame, whom Janice decided to name after her grandfather. However, before the birth of Kwame, Jack had to report to Parris Island for basic training. He would eventually miss the birth of his son, but he was happy when he came home after basic training to find a healthy little boy who looked just like him.

After an honorable discharge from the United States marines, Jack decided to go back to Brooklyn to be with his family. Kwame was only four years old when his father finally came home for good. Jack was a proud father, who dreamed about offering the world to his son. Jack was in the midst of joining the New York Fire Department when a tragedy hit him. He had gone through all the preliminary exams and was cleared to become a part of the fire department. All Jack needed to do was to pass the grueling physical exam. Whenever he thought about the future of his family, he smiled at the thought of finally being able to give them a life better than his. Kwame was the pride and joy of his father and there was nothing in the world that Jack wouldn't do to ensure a better life for his boy and his wife. While Janice held her job as a teacher's assistant to help hold down the family until Jack started his new job, the family was hopeful about the future and they wanted to celebrate their good fortune. Having grown up in the Brownsville projects, Jack had left his wife and baby back there when he joined the US marines. Of course, he never saw a long-term life in the projects, but there was no other choice at the time. Janice also grew up in the same housing projects. Once Jack received word that he was only a physical away from becoming a member of the New York Fire Department, he decided to take his wife out to celebrate that evening.

The mood was festive when Jack arrived home earlier that day. He bought a dozen roses from the Mexican guy who sold flowers on Rockaway and Pitkin Avenue in Brooklyn. He wasn't being cheap or anything like that; it was just convenient to buy the fresh flowers a couple of blocks away from his home. He met his wife and son at the door with the roses in hand. Janice was happy to see her handsome husband home, and she wondered why he was so happy. "Are these roses for me?" she asked sarcastically. "No, they're for my other woman," Jack told her playfully. "The only other woman you better have better be your mother," she said with a jealous tone. "Of course, the roses are for you, Baby," he said while his lips met hers for a kiss. Four year-old Kwame ran to his dad for a hug. Kwame was a little tired, so Jack took him to the living room and rocked him to sleep. After falling asleep shortly thereafter, Jack took his son to his room and put him down for a late afternoon nap. He was a proud daddy as he stood above the single bed to watch his son's angelic face in a deep sleep.

Meanwhile, Janice was in the kitchen trying to fix Jack a snack. "I'm making you a sandwich, babe. I know you probably need a snack before dinner," she yelled from the kitchen. Jack got up from the couch and walked to the kitchen. He got behind his wife and held her from the back while whispering, "The only snack I need right now is you, babe." Janice smiled and said, "You want your son to walk in here to find his daddy snacking on his mother?" Jack smiled while telling her, "I already put my boy to sleep. It's just me and you right now. Besides, don't even worry about making dinner tonight, because I'm taking you out to eat. Maybe we can get my mother to watch Kwame for the night," he suggested. "That sounds good. What do you have in mind?" she asked. "Well, right now, the only thing I have in mind is to take you on this counter," he told her while grinning. Janice immediately recognized that look of hunger on her husband's face and she couldn't wait to serve it to him on a platter on the kitchen counter.

The tantalizing rub of Janice's stomach by Jack while he stood behind his wife, only intensified the rush of blood down to his crotch. The natural scientific growth of his ten-inch snake against Janice's butt was hard to resist. She turned to face him and was amused by the fact that her husband was so easily turned on by her, even when she was in the kitchen barefoot, wearing a doo rag on her head, reminiscent of Aunt Jemima. Jack had moved beyond the physical beauty of his wife. She was his other half and he felt whole in her presence. After giving birth to his one and only child, Jack was over the hill, not just for his wife, but his entire family. She was the sexiest woman on earth, to him. Her natural beauty radiated under the soft light in the kitchen, and her smile continued to melt his heart. He flashed his pearly whites as he allowed her to gaze into his eyes, feeling the greatness of her man and the good life he had outlined for them. Jack's chiseled body was desired by many of the women who lived in his building, but he knew his heart belonged to his one and only, Janice. His strong cheeks, medium dark complexion, broad nose, full lips, big oval eyes, thick eyebrows and clef chin fit perfectly on his well-shaven face. Jack embodied great physical fitness. Janice couldn't believe her eyes when her husband returned home from the Marines. He especially looked sexy to her while wearing his uniform.

Even after bearing her first child, Janice's body snapped right back into place, but with a few more curves added, to Jack's delight. Her petite frame at 5ft 2inches with a 24inch waist, 34 inch hips, perky C cups, made Janice the desire of most men, whenever her presence graced the streets to walk to the store. Her dark and lovely complexion, shoulder length hair, button nose, bright eyes and oval face combined to make her a physical threat to any woman within her vicinity. Some of the drug dealers took delight in watching her come and go from her apartment, but Janice didn't care about their existence or admiration for her. Jack was her hero and her heart and she could never be swayed from him.

While an impatient Jack was kissing his wife in the kitchen and contemplating whether or not the countertop in the kitchen was the best place to entice her into a late afternoon snack, Janice helped ease his decision by whispering in his ear, "I miss you, Baby. I want you to take me right now." The position or place in the kitchen was irrelevant to Jack at that moment, because all he cared about was to follow his wife's directives. He soon lifted her off her feet and placed her on the edge of the counter in the kitchen. Janice leaned back enough so her head could rest on the back wall while her legs spread apart so Jack could enjoy the aroma of her Garden of Eden. He eased her underwear down her legs with his teeth while savoring her moisture through the fabric. He then began to passionately kiss his wife for what seemed endless. As their lips finally parted ways, Jack decided to maneuver his tongue down to her braless breasts as she allowed the straps of her muumuu to fall off her shoulders for easy access. Jack found his wife irresistible even while she was wearing a muumuu. Her bouncy breasts were delicious as he took her nipples in his mouth and sucked gently on them. While Jack's tongue was magical, Janice couldn't contain her excitement. "Oooh, Baby. It's been so long. I want you to take me," she uttered while Jack was trying his best to be patient with her.

      Jack never intended to have a quickie with his wife, but a quickie it would be this time, for Janice. Jack's bedroom skills and the thorough knowledge of his wife's body had never diminished. He knew exactly what to do to take her to ecstasy. He quickly maneuvered his head down towards her crotch, as she let herself go, expecting to climax within seconds of his touch. Jack quickly surveyed her stomach area with his tongue before making his way down to her clitoris. She grabbed on to his bald pate before holding in her scream of ecstasy. In an effort to keep Kwame from waking up, Janice sounded as if she was sulking while her husband forced a nut out of her. Tears of love dropped from Janice's face as she realized how much she was in love with her husband. Noticing her emotional state, Jack quickly grabbed her and wrapped her legs around him while penetrating her sugar walls on the way to the couch in the living room. He had unfastened his own belt and dropped his underwear and pants while he licked her to heaven. He was deep inside of her as she held on to him tightly to allow his manhood to fulfill her. "I miss you so much, Baby," he whispered to his wife, while carrying on a heavenly rhythm that his wife was enjoying. "I miss you too, Baby. Make it sweet, Babe," she suggested. Slowing down his movement to allow his wife the goodness of his strokes, Jack started smiling as his wife closed her eyes for what was near. "Oh baby, I'm about to come again," she said faintly. "I'm gonna come with you, Babe," he told her as he stroked her a few more times. Janice was happy that her husband had finally come home for good. They were going to be the family she always dreamed of.

A Hero Gone

Jack's mother showed up later that evening to relieve them for the night so Jack could celebrate the new possibilities in his life with his wife. Grandma was more than happy to babysit her one and only grandson. Jack was also her favorite child and the only son she ever had. Jack's mother had a total of five children, but none of them had the drive and determination that Jack had. The other four daughters all had children and they were all girls. Jack was elated when his mother showed up, as he had made plans to take his wife to Manhattan and treat her to a nice dinner. At the time, one of the hottest restaurants in Manhattan was the Motown Café and Janice had always wanted to go there. Jack was happy to oblige his wife. Since the early fall weather was nice and breezy, Jack decided to wear a pair of gray wool pants, light burgundy cotton shirt, black shoes, black belt and a black blazer. He also sprayed the back of his ears and neck with a little of Calvin Klein's Obsession cologne. His scent alone drove Janice nuts. She just smiled, because her husband looked so good to her. Janice whipped out a special little black dress that she bought while Jack was away in the service. She was holding on to it just for a special occasion with her husband. It was a merino one-shoulder dress that accentuated her every curve. She wore over-the-knee suede boots to accent the dress. The sweet smell of Chanel #5 invaded Jack's nostrils when she stepped in the room. And he just looked at his wife and felt proud.

The handsome couple looked lovely and was happy as they left the house to head to Manhattan for dinner. Jack decided to take a livery cab to the train station for the easy ride to Manhattan. They arrived on 53rd street around 7:00pm for dinner. Janice ordered all her favorite southern dishes; macaroni and cheese, greens, white rice and black beans, and smothered pork chops. Jack ate whatever his wife ordered. The two of them were just getting caught up at dinner. It was the best conversation they had in a while. Dinner was delicious and the couple enjoyed the moment they were spending together. It had been a while since Jack and Janice had gone anywhere together. This dinner sort of rekindled their romance and they seemed like they were falling in love all over again. After dinner, they took a stroll down to Time Square holding hands like two teenagers in love. While showing each other a little PDA (public display of affection) in Time Square, Jack and Janice got a little hot with each other. They realized they needed to head home so they could end the night passionately. They ran down to the train station to catch the 3 train back to Brooklyn.

On the ride back to Brooklyn, Jack and Janice were flirting and being playful with each other. A few vagrants tried to intervene, but Jack's demeanor was enough to send them on their way. His military toughness and intimidating look was enough to ward off any potential attacker. The couple finally made it to their stop on Sutter Avenue and couldn't wait to get home to have a little fun with each other. After reaching the street, Jack and Janice found it difficult to get a cab. Jack understood the risk of walking a few blocks to his home, but he had no choice after waiting for close to fifteen minutes and no livery cab ever came. Janice was a little apprehensive about the walk herself, but she said nothing to her strong man. Jack had served a couple of tours of duty in Iraq and made it out safely, so Brooklyn was a cake walk to him, so he thought.

Since the weather wasn't so brisk and the distance to his house was a little less than ten blocks, Jack decided to take the long stroll with his wife. The conversation was flowing and the couple was happy about their hopeful future. They were so hopeful that Jack forgot about his surroundings and let his guard down without realizing it. He was just two blocks from his home when two men approached him. "Kick in your wallet," one of the men said, while brandishing a gun on his waist. Jack tried to stare the man down and show that he didn't fear him. He stood still while holding his wife's hand tightly. "Kick in your muthafucking wallet, punk," the other man said as he pulled out a shiny 9mm handgun. Jack didn't want to jeopardize his or his wife's life, but he could tell he was in great danger. The two men could tell that Jack was no soft punk and robbing him would come with dire consequences. "You sure you wanna do this?" Jack asked firmly without showing any trepidation. Janice stayed silent, while the episode unfolded. "Muthafucka, you wanna be superman in front of your woman? Kick in your muthafucking wallet before I bust a cap in your ass," the initial guy said. Jack could read the fear in the eyes of both men. He eased his hand in his pocket, pulled his wallet out and handed it to the man. Janice thought her husband did the right thing by giving up his wallet and they were halfway home, safely. However, the two men were not satisfied. While rummaging through Jack's wallet to find the forty dollars left in it, they ran across his military ID. "Who do we have here, G.I. muthafucking Joe," one of them said, after pulling the military ID out of the wallet. "Well, G.I. Joe, forty dollars ain't gonna cut it. Kick in your wedding rings, your watch and every fucking thing you have on you," the other robber said, while holding the gun to Jack's head.

Jack thought perhaps if he was alone, the outcome of the situation would've been different because he would've reacted differently, but due to the safety of his wife, he was willing to honor every request the stick-up kids made. He took off his watch and wedding ring and handed them over to the robbers. "We want your bitch's ring, too, muthafucka," one of them yelled. Submitting to a couple of punks was one thing, but allowing them to disrespect his wife, while trying to emasculate him would only go so far. "There's no reason to disrespect my wife. I gave you everything you asked for. There's not gonna be any more calling my wife a bitch," Jack said sternly. "This muthafucka must think he Rambo or something. What the fuck are you gonna do if I call your bitch a bitch. She a bitch, chump," one of them said, while waving his gun in Jack's face. Jack could tell they didn't know how to handle a gun from the way they were holding the guns. He didn't want the situation to escalate, but he knew the two men were too scared to let him go about his business. He was trying to figure out a way to subdue one of them in order for him to have a surviving chance with his wife.

Instead of trying to make their getaway, the two robbers wanted to instigate Jack and denigrate his wife further. It only took one more time for them to call his wife a bitch before he disarmed one of them and shot him in the head. The other man started shooting as he took off running, but Jack was shot in the stomach as he jumped in front of his wife to shield her from the assailant's bullet, but not before he let off three shots that hit the running assailant, two in the back and one in his head. Jack would've had a surviving chance if the police department and medics responded in time, but it took twenty minutes for the ambulance and the cops to get to the scene, and Jack bled to death on the way to the hospital.

That tragedy would ultimately change the lives of Janice and her son Kwame, but another surprise was on the way nine months later. After Jack's death, Janice found out she was pregnant with her second child, a baby girl. She named the healthy baby girl Jacqueline Robinson, after her dad, but everyone in the family called her Jackie. Janice's fate as a single mother was decided by two gunmen on a night when she and her husband were celebrating a better future. Jack had done tours of duty in Iraq and came home unscathed every time, but it took two bad apples in his own country and neighborhood to take his life.

Kwame was the spitting image of his dad, a man he never got to know well enough beyond the extent that he was his daddy at four years old. After Jack came home, he spent most of his time with his son, and Kwame acted as if his dad was one of his favorite superheroes. Whenever Jack came home for the holidays, he made his family a priority and organized special outings, so he could spend time with them. This time, he was home permanently and he wanted to do what his father didn't do, stick around to help his mother raise him. Alas, a male role model is one of the hardest things to find in the black community, Kwame came that to learn as a man.

Grandma's Love

Janice was a wreck for many months after the death of her husband. She feared her neighborhood more than ever before. Even a short trip to the supermarket to go grocery shopping was a nightmare for Janice. She did not know whether or not the assailants' family had planned to retaliate for the two men that Jack shot. The wrecking of her nerves almost caused her to have a breakdown. It was time for her grandmother to step in and offer the help that Janice so desperately needed. Grandma Jones finally decided to step in to help her granddaughter with her children. Grandma Jones' husband had died a few years earlier and she lived alone in a three-bedroom house located on Sutter Avenue, a couple of blocks away from Brownsville projects. Though she tried her best to encourage her son, Janice's father, to become more than a statistic, he fell victim to the trappings of the hood and found himself doing a 20-year bid for drug distribution. Grandma Jones vowed never to walk in that prison to go see her son, because she raised him better than that.

She figured the least she could do was to help her grandchild and her great grandchildren while they were in distress. Not that grandma was on her death bed at the ripe old age of eighty, but she knew that father time would eventually catch up to her. Having raised her four children with her husband, she now wanted to spend the rest of her golden years enjoying her great grandchildren. Kwame loved his great grandmother dearly and she was nuts about her first great-grandchild. Grandma offered to have Janice move into her house, along with Kwame. Then Jackie had not been born yet, but she was due soon. Janice was very grateful that her grandmother had offered to help. She accepted her help without hesitation. The last thing Janice wanted to do was to raise her children in a place their daddy had died. Janice packed her belongings and said goodbye to the projects, but her mother stayed there because that was where she had raised her children since the conviction of their father. As much as Janice wanted to take her mother along with her to her grandmother's house, grandma wanted none of it. Janice's mom had never gotten along with her paternal grandmother. Grandma always blamed Janice's mom for derailing her son's future. It was because of the beautiful girl with the hazel eyes that he decided to drop out of college to have a family. That family ultimately forced him into selling drugs because his wife wanted the finer things in life. He was grandma's favorite child and probably the smartest of all her children. He was dubbed to be the first physician in the family because of his wonderful brain. However, grandma's favorite son would never make it to the heights of the expectations set for him. He went to college, met a girl who was visiting and they developed a relationship. He hadn't even completed his first year in college when Janice's mom became pregnant with Janice. Grandma was mad as hell, and took out her anger and frustration on Janice's mom. It took the birth of her granddaughter for grandma to even utter a kind word to Janice's mom. However, she could never let go of the resentment she held towards her.

This time around, grandma wanted to do things a little differently, though history was repeating itself in her family. Since her granddaughter continued the cycle of having children without completing college, it was up to grandma to end the cycle of resenting her children for making mistakes in life. She decided she would help Janice, but only if she promised to continue to go to school to get her degree. Grandma did the best she could to help assist with the children, but she was getting old and she was limited as far as her assistance. Janice, however, was grateful and she eventually did as promised, and completed her college degree. As a little boy, Kwame was very attentive to his great grandmother and he kept her company throughout most of her days. She loved that boy with all her heart. There was no lack of love for Jackie from grandma, but Kwame reminded her of her own son whose middle name was also Kwame. She spoiled the boy so much, sometimes Janice felt threatened by her.

It wasn't until grandma's passing that everyone realized how much she really loved her great-grandson. Almost her entire estate was left to Kwame, including the house. All the money that grandma had saved while she worked, along with the insurance money from her dead husband, she used to establish a college fund for Kwame and Jackie. She also had a clause in her will that if they decided not to attend college that the money should then be given to her favorite charity in honor of her name. Grandma was specific in her will. She wanted none of her children to have anything of hers, because she felt she and her husband had given the best opportunities to all of them when they reared them from birth. Since Jackie and Kwame were the only great-grandchildren and all of her grandchildren were adults, she decided to set a better future for the great-grandchildren instead. Grandma was more calculated than everyone in the family gave her credit for. Most of her children had started fighting over who was going to get what when she died, but in the end, she didn't feel that any of them deserved anything. Her will also caused a rift within the family, because on paper it appeared as if Janice was the only one who inherited anything from grandma through her children.

Kwame took it hard when his nana died, but he realized he had to be strong for his mother because in some kind of unofficial way, he became the man of the house. Taking on the role of the man of the house forced Kwame to be a lot more responsible and mature than his peers. He had to become his mother's keeper. Though Janice was a young mom, she was very stern and made sure her son was disciplined and respectful. Those qualities would later help steer Kwame in the right direction in his life.

Grandma's Tale

Before her passing, Kwame spent most of his time with his favorite person in the world, his great grandma, at home as a youngster. It was his grandma who decided one day to tell him about his family's history. She wasn't in the best of health at the time, but Grandma Jones wanted to make sure that her great grandson knew his proud heritage. Though her voice was cracking at times, Grandma Jones told Kwame the family's history dating back to his great-great-great-grandfather. In as loving a voice as a grandma could, she began, "Your bloodline came from one of the purest warrior tribes in Ghana, Africa from the Ashanti Empire. Your great-great-great-grandfather was part of the most powerful military group in Ghana. Men like your great-great-great-grandfather with the Ashanti bloodline are natural leaders and warriors. And you are, too, baby.

The word Ghana itself translates to warrior king. The Ashanti Empire from 1701 to 1896 was a West African state of the Ashanti people, the Akan people of the Ashanti Region, now in Ghana. The Ashanti are a major ethnic group in Ghana, a powerful, militaristic and highly disciplined people of West Africa that your forefathers belonged to. Their strategic effective

military power came from an early adoption of European rifles that helped create an empire that stretched from central Ghana to present day Togo and Ivory Coast, bordered by the Dagomba kingdom to the north and Dahomey to the east. Due to the empire's military prowess, sophisticated hierarchy, social stratification and culture, the Ashanti Empire had one of the largest historiographies of any indigenous sub-Saharan African political entity. Today the Ashanti monarchy continues as a constitutionally protected, sub-national traditional state in the Republic of Ghana."
Grandma Jones became thirsty in the midst of the story, so Kwame walked to the kitchen to get her a glass of water. "Was my great-great-great-grandpa a fearless fighter in Africa, grandma?" Kwame asked with curiosity. "Well, come sit down and I'll tell you the rest of the story, baby," Grandma Jones told him, while pointing to a warm spot next to her on the couch. She continued, "In the early eighteenth century your great-great-great-grandfather, a very feared captain in the Ghanaian army, was betrayed by one of his closest friends for money and sold into slavery to a United States slave-trader after his capture. Your great-great-great-grandfather was relentless about his freedom. He knew he didn't belong on anybody's cotton field or plantation, so he plotted his escape from his master the very first day they brought him to the plantation and every day thereafter. Faced with so many obstacles, including a language barrier from his fellow slaves who

were captured from other parts of Africa, your great-great-great-grandfather attempted his first escape alone. While looking in the distance, he thought he could disappear through the corn fields without being noticed. That was the worst mistake he could've made. Another slave who was trying to get in the good graces of the master, noticed he was gone and reported him instantly. These are the slaves that were called house Negroes. They used to kiss the master's ass in order to get in their good graces. Perhaps that slave could've been jealous of the fact that your great-great-great-grandfather, whose Ghanaian name was Kwaku, was much closer to freedom than he ever was. History would never tell it. However, your great-great-great-grandfather suffered the worst punishment after he was captured and brought back to the plantation. He was tied to a boulder, stripped naked while the overseer whipped him with a lasso in front of the other slaves. The welts on his back alone were a scary enough reminder of what would happen to any other slave who tried to escape from the plantation."

"Did my grandpa die, grandma?" Kwame asked sadly. "It would take more than that to kill your great grandpa. He was a strong man. The white folks had taken away your great-great-great-grandfather's identity and African name when he first arrived to America, but they couldn't away his will and pride. Because he was so big compared to the rest of the men, they started calling him Big, but after his first escape attempt through the woods, they started calling him Mountain Man and the name stuck until his death, though his original name was Kwaku Kwame Opoku. The name Kwaku came from the Ashanti tribe and was given to him because he was born on Wednesday. However, to recognize his mother's Akan bloodline, that's your great-great-great-great-grandmother, your great-great-great-granddaddy was given the middle name Kwame, also because his mother was born on Saturday. As it is tradition for Ghanaian people to name their children based on the day of the week that they are born, the name Kwaku was given to your great-great-great-grandfather.

Kwame intently listened with anticipation. "This here gonna be a long story, baby, but you gonna like it," grandma told him. She continued, "Not afraid of the whippings he received at the order of his master, Kwaku would try escaping again and each time he was captured his punishment was more severe. It took some time before he realized that he had to devise a master plan and strategize his escape by becoming friends with his enemies. Kwaku became the hardest working slave on the field in the next few years while mapping out his escape route. This time he vowed not to be caught alive and there would be a lot of bloodshed on his way to freedom. White folks often underestimate the resilience of African folks, even today. And despite the fact that black people have been through so much, we still stand strong today and will continue to stand strong until the end of time. White people have yet to figure out that we cannot be broken. Unlike the annihilation of all the Indians, black people have survived the most atrocious situations." Before grandma could continue, Kwame had a question, "What's ah-nah-la-tion, grandma?" Grandma smiled because of the mispronunciation of the word by her great grandson, but she gave him a brief meaning of the word, 'Annihilation is when something is destroyed completely.' Many of these lessons and stories were passed on from Kwame's great-great-great-grandfather all the way down to his grandmother, his mother and then to him. "Your great-great-great-granddaddy was a survivor and a relentless fighter. He dreamed about having a wife and children like most human beings, but most of all, he dreamed of having free children, and freedom had to start with him. He risked his life to make our lives better," his grandma told him.

Though the story was long, Kwame found it interesting and captivating. His grandma had his full attention, "It had been a few years since Kwaku's capture from his homeland, but he never gave up hope that he would be a free man again. While he gained the trust of the overseer and master, he also befriended another newly arrived slave who was just as frustrated as he was with captivity. The new slave had also attempted to escape and was caught and beaten close to death by the overseer. An example had to be made out of him to show the new slaves what their fate would be if escaping even crossed their minds. The two formed a secret friendship, but acted as if they hated each other around the other house Negroes on the plantation. One time they even had to settle their differences with closed fists while entertaining the master. Though Kwaku and his new friend didn't want to fight each other, they knew they had to put on a good show for the master. Once they realized it was confirmed that they hated each other, it was time to move forward with their plan to escape. Kwaku's plan to act alone was not gonna work. He knew he stood a better chance of fighting if he had a trusted, fearless partner he could count on." Grandma made the story interesting enough so that Kwame wasn't bored. However, 99% of what she told him was true.

Grandma was a great storyteller and she would pause to emphasize her points and to move on to the next phase of the story. She continued, "There was more than one overseer on the plantation and their sleeping quarters was a rock throw away from the shanty shacks that the slaves called home. These shacks were equipped with subhuman amenities. The floors were clay dirt and the walls were wooden framed with dirt mortar and a straw roof. The master, however, lived in a lavish home away from the slaves with more than enough amenities befitting for a king than needed. The overseers lived in a wood cabin with a tin roof and a cement floor, which was much better than the slave quarters. It seemed like the overseers took pleasure in beating the slaves and controlling them. One particular overseer was especially mean to the slaves because one of the daughters of the master had reported to him that his weewee wasn't half the size of most of the slaves. He and the young lady were having an affair, but the young lady seemed a little too overzealous about the taste of chocolate, to him. You know those jezebels love to taste the black man. He wanted to punish the slaves and emasculate them because of his own insecurities." There were a few words that Kwame didn't understand, such as jezebel, chocolate, and emasculate, but grandma simplified them all for him. At twelve years old, Kwame was very bright and advanced, so he was able to follow along. "Kwaku happened to be taking a pee by the sycamore tree located on the hill behind the plantation when the young pristine looking master's daughter appeared. "Oh my God! Is that really all you?" she asked with curiosity upon setting her eyes on Kwaku's weewee. Fearing the wrath of what could possibly bestowed upon him if the overseer caught him exposing himself to the young lady, Kwaku took off running while wrapping his package back into his pants. She ran after him. "No need to be scared. I'm not gonna hurt you. It's just that I've never seen a penis so big," she told him. Kwaku was a little timid and he also knew that he couldn't be caught talking to that young woman, because it would be a death sentence. "I think you should be goin' now, ma'am," he told her, with the limited English he had acquired from being on the plantation. The young woman looked around to survey the area before telling Kwaku, "There's nobody here. I just wanna see it up close." Kwaku was on the verge of running towards the slave quarters, away from this crazy white woman before he got killed. However, before he could take off, she threatened to tell her daddy that he was trying to rape her if he didn't honor her request. "Billy Bob's weewee is not even half the size of yours. And he think he's doing something when we're doing it," she revealed to Kwaku. Kwaku hadn't yet grasped the gist of the whole conversation, but he was scared to death. This girl was habitual with her request to see the slaves' weewees. The last time Billy Bob caught her looking at an unwilling slave's weewees, the slave was hung on the sycamore tree. Kwaku was a witness to his death. That's all he took from the situation and that was enough to instill fear in him since he became a slave." Grandma was telling a fascinating story and Kwame was all ears.

Grandma was trying her best to keep the language age appropriate for the story, but sometimes she was so angry she had to say what she wanted. "Billy Bob was the meanest of the three SOB overseers on the plantation and he had been sleeping with the master's daughter since her little "too hot to trot" ass reached puberty. Billy Bob called it love, while the girl was only doing it for the thrill. Since her father was very strict and gave her very little time to interact with kids her own age at school, Billy Bob was her next best option. She was dropped to school every morning and picked up immediately when school was over by Billy Bob. It even took a while before her father trusted Billy Bob enough to allow him to go pick her up from school every day in the chariot. "Come on now, you're gonna let me see your weewee or am I gonna have to tell Billy Bob that you were making a pass at his woman?" she threatened Kwaku again. Kwaku thought about the consequences of not flashing his johnson to this white girl and became overly frightful. Pictures of himself hung on a tree, flashed before his eyes. He had seen the live hangings of many other slaves before and that picture never left his mind. After being caught a few times after failed escapes, Kwaku knew that he was wearing out his chances on the plantation to live. He reluctantly pulled his johnson out while the white girl salivated over its size," grandma and Kwame had grown comfortable with each other over the years, but talking about johnsons was not something she envisioned ever doing with her great grandson, but it was part of the story.

"You happy, miss? Ok. Goodbye," he said as he ran off to the slave quarters after allowing the white girl to get a glimpse of his johnson. That episode with the master's daughter hunted Kwaku for a long time and caused many sleepless nights and nightmares for him. Many a night, he would wake up in cold sweats after having a nightmare about being hung publicly for showing his johnson to this white girl. As bad as things were in Kwaku's mind, they were about to get worse. The white girl was not satisfied with just seeing his johnson anymore, now she also wanted to get a taste of it. At the time, the corporal punishment for a black man fornicating with a white girl was death, and that law was on the books. Doing it with the master's daughter on his own plantation? The punishment for that was torture until death. This white girl knew she was playing with fire and Kwaku knew that she was not worth his life. He was still fighting to get his freedom and now there was one more obstacle for him to deal with," grandma was getting a little tired and sleepy herself, so she decided to summarize the rest of the story for Kwame. However, Kwame would later interpret the rest of the story his own way.

According to Kwame's mature imagination, the master's daughter, Ms. Mary Lou, wanted nothing more than to taste Kwaku's big Johnson. She dreamed about sleeping with a big black slave with a big johnson. The evident moisture between her legs as she tossed and turn in the middle of the night while steady humping the pillow held between her legs was becoming unbearable. She was tired of psychologically sexing the big black slave with the big penis. She wanted the real thing and she would stop at nothing until Kwaku gave her a taste. At 17 years old, Mary Lou was cunning, conniving and luscious at the same time. Her voluptuous breasts, flawless skin, deep blue eyes and long flowing hair made her the pride of her mom and dad. She was going to marry the boy down the street whose parents owned a plantation bigger than her father's. As a matter of fact, she was being groomed for it. She attended etiquette classes with many other girls her age, so she could end up with a good husband from a rich family like hers. Mary Lou played the role of a good southern belle perfectly. Her parents had no idea that she had lost her virginity to Billy Bob. Even though he was a white boy, Billy Bob would have been shot by her father if it was ever revealed that he had taken Mary Lou's virginity. He was the help and the master did not want his daughter to end up with the help.

    Mary Lou was a spoiled little brat who always got her way. Her daddy was very influential around town and he was adored because he had introduced most of the plantation owners to the new way of turning a hostile slave to docile. Kwaku was one of the examples that he used to show off his skills as a slave-maker. Mary Lou could pretty much do whatever she wanted and nobody would say anything to her. However, she was treading dangerous water this time, trying to get a slave to have sex with her. This was an unforgivable sin and her daddy could downright disown her for it if he found out. Mary Lou was smart enough to know that her daddy would never believe that she would initiate any sexual relation with a slave. Her plan was to yell "rape!" if she got caught. Kwaku may have been caught a few times while trying to escape the plantation, but he also was not as dumb as they believed. Another possible problem Mary Lou faced if she got caught, her parents would definitely ship her out of town because she would be marked as damaged goods for having been with a slave whether through rape or voluntarily. She thought long and hard about the consequences of her actions, but the lust in her eyes and between her thighs for the black Mandingo clouded her judgment. Mary Lou had to have a taste of the chocolate. It was after she tasted Kwaku's goods that she became addicted and Kwaku ended up using her addiction to him as a way to escape.

The Great Escape

The master initially didn't even trust the white boy overseer to take Mary Lou to school, but he damn near had a heart attack when she requested to be taken to school by Kwaku and Luol. She was able to explain her request to him by having her father believe that she needed to show the white boy's family that she was "supposed" to marry that her family had enough money and the strongest slaves in town. Her father's narcissistic nature allowed him to believe it and soon, Kwaku and Luol, were taking and picking up the missy from school every day. It was her way to spend more time with Kwaku away from her dad. Honestly, the only reason why her father even allowed Kwaku and Luol to take her to school was because of the "rift" between Kwaku and Luol. Supposedly, Luol was supposed to report to the master everything and anything that Kwaku did wrong, but in reality, Kwaku and Luol had set up the situation exactly as they wanted so they could escape. In front of the white folks and other slaves, Kwaku and Luol couldn't stand each other, but behind closed doors they were partners. They had worked hard to gain the trust of the master. Kwaku had already been on the plantation for close to ten years, so he acted as if he resigned to his fate as a slave indefinitely. Luol did the same thing, with the exception that he became an ass kisser and an uncle Tom, in the eyes of the other slaves. He sacrificed his dignity for almost eight years so he could gain his freedom. He was always the lookout for the master and the overseers. There wasn't a rumor that Luol couldn't start to gain the trust of the white folks.

Meanwhile, little Ms. Pretty was falling head over heels for the big black slave. She knew she couldn't be with him openly, so she created ways to see him in the middle of the night, on the way to and from school. One time she even forced Luol to serve as a lookout while she went in the woods with Kwaku on the way back from school. She even threatened to tell her dad Luol raped her if he said anything about the affair with Kwaku. Luol saw it as nothing more than a step closer to his freedom. He and Kwaku had been planning for years and they couldn't wait to execute their plan.

The day to execute their plan was nearing and Kwaku wanted to make sure he was ready. He had talked Mary Lou into getting two of her father's shotguns with a couple of boxes of bullets for him, by asking her to teach him how to shoot. She took the two guns out of the gun case the night before and placed them on the back of the chariot, along with the bullets. She threw a cover over them to hide them from the overseers and her dad. Kwaku was always the first to go get the chariot in the morning so he could take her to school. Most people in town had gotten used to seeing Kwaku and Luol around town driving Mary Lou around. However, on this particular day, Kwaku and Luol never intended to go back to the field to work. They had heard about a place called Pennsylvania in the north and they wanted to make sure they made it there. It usually took them about an hour to bring Mary Lou to school and come back, and Kwaku figured he would have about an hour headstart on the trackers if he took off right after he dropped her off. Having been in the military when he was in Ghana helped him figure out the map to Pennsylvania with no problem. Kwaku and Luol decided to go through the woods and shallow rivers in order to keep from being tracked by dogs. It took them almost a week to make it from Alabama to Pennsylvania while riding almost nonstop, as they took turns sleeping, but they made it and picked up a few other slaves on the way. By the time they reached Virginia, they had shot and killed at least six white people who questioned their status as freed slaves. As far as they were concerned slavery was a thing of the past and only death could keep them from freedom.

When the group of newly arrived slaves set foot on the soils of Pennsylvania, they decided to break up to avoid suspicion. The chariot was broken down and most of them ended up trekking the rest of the way by foot until they ran into other black people who offered to help them get settled. Back then, most of the free slaves in the north opened their homes to the newly arrived slaves to help them get on their feet, as long as they were willing to help harvest the land. Kwaku and Luol decided to part ways when they reached Pennsylvania. Each of them kept one of the shotguns while trying to find their way to civilization.

A New Settlement

After finally escaping from the plantation to Pennsylvania, the first state to abolish slavery in 1780, though Vermont was the first territory to do so in 1777, Kwaku met a an established black family that took him in and he taught them the most effective way to harvest their land. It was in Pennsylvania while trying to establish himself as a free citizen that Kwaku met his wife while working as a farmer for the black family. Kwaku's skills as a farmer were so advanced that he helped double the family's harvest the first year. Kwaku's dream of being a free man was realized and he worked relentlessly to create a family and assimilate into a culture that was still foreign to him. Though he longed to return back home to Ghana, Kwaku found that life in Pennsylvania wasn't as hard as the life he once had as a captive slave in Alabama. Kwaku and his wife eventually had seven children, five boys and two girls. One of his sons was named Kwame and fought with the first black infantry in New York known as the Buffalo Soldiers during the Civil War.

Kwame was one of a few lucky black men to return home safely after the war. However, after serving his time with his brigade, he decided to settle in New York City where he met a beautiful girl and married. The couple had four children, but most of Kwame's fortune was eventually stolen from him because of prejudice and racist laws that prevented him from land ownership and full citizenship in this country. Though American by birth and a veteran of the United States Army, Kwame never received the treatment he deserved as a war hero and was never recognized for his bravery by the United States government. He left all of his possessions and wealth that he had accumulated to his four children when he passed. One of his daughters, Janice's grandmother, would eventually buy a house in the Brownsville section of Brooklyn and that house has remained in the family ever since.

The Young Man

A loner since middle school, Kwame was always intelligent and deviated from the norm at an early age. Nobody in his neighborhood dreamed about becoming a Navy SEAL, but Kwame wasn't the average teenager. Considered a weirdo by most people as a kid for the way that he dressed, he learned to be self-reliant by spending his spare time studying the martial arts. Kwame was one of many victims of a fatherless household. His mother, Janice, tried her best to raise her son to be a man, but Kwame would find his male role model at the dojo in his teacher, Kevin. He taught Kwame how to deal with his emotions and anger, but most of all, he taught him discipline. Kwame was also a great student of the martial arts. He moved through the ranks in no time. By the time he reached sophomore year in high school, he had earned his black belt in karate.

Kwame tried his best to go through his daily life without any problems. He wanted to one day become a karate instructor to pass on the great teachings of his teacher Kevin. However, Kwame's patience would be tested by the popular high school bully and thug, during his junior year. No one knew of his martial arts training, but Kwame wore his sweats to school most of the time because it was easier for him to make it to the dojo for practice every day from school. While walking the halls on the way to his next class, Michael, the well-known thug of the school who practically robbed every student at the school of their lunch money at one time or another, confronted Kwame while his gang looked on. "Hey weirdo, where's my lunch money for today?" he asked. Kwame kept walking and acted like he wasn't being addressed. Michael hurried to cut him off. "Didn't you hear me talking to you?" he shoved Kwame on his chest. "Look, I don't want any problems with you guys. I'm just trying to get to my next class," Kwame said. "Not before I get my lunch money for today, punk," Michael reached in to smack Kwame. However, Kwame's natural reflex caught Michael's hand before it could reach his face, and with the strength of a bull, Kwame started bending Michael's fingers until he begged for mercy in pain. Each time one of his goons tried to get closer to help assist him, Kwame would press harder on Michael's fingers, forcing him to call off members of his crew. By the time Kwame let go of his hand, the assistant principal was making his way around the corner and screamed to them, "Get to class! The bell is about to ring!"

Like most bullies, Michael had a point to prove to his crew and a beat-down for Kwame was imminent. Armed with a twelve-inch knife and ten flunkies around him to protect him in case he couldn't handle himself in a duel, Michael set out to even the score with

Kwame after school. The embarrassment he suffered at the hands of Kwame earlier in the day was enough for his flunkies to question his leadership and heart. He needed to prove to them that he was a great leader and that no one was going to get away with embarrassing him or anybody from his crew. Michael's reputation preceded him. He had never lost a fight to anyone at the high school and he wasn't going to allow Kwame the first W. Honestly, Michael had never had a fair fight in his life. A sucker-punch or completely blindsiding his opponent with a bottle across the face or a bat at the knees had been his ammo in the past. A fair fight to Michael was when he and his crew of almost ten guys beat another crew of two or three people.

Meanwhile, Kwame wasn't even thinking about Michael as he went about his day, hoping to make it to karate practice in time after school. Finally, the last bell rang and it was time to get out of school. Frederick Douglas Academy High had its history of troubled youths, but none had been as serious as Michael. As Kwame made his way down the block, Michael and his gang emerged and surrounded him. "What you gonna do now, chump?" Michael shoved Kwame on the chest again. Kwame spun around to assess his situation and his chances of victory against a gang of more than ten guys. The odds weren't in his favor, but his teacher also told him that odds didn't always matter, odds could also be changed. The element of surprise is always relevant and attacking an opponent or the enemy at the right time with the right combination of power can change those odds at any moment.

Very common of chumps, Michael started talking loudly to attract a crowd, and within seconds, a group of kids from the school gathered around to witness the next beat-down, courtesy of Michael. It was street cinema at its best, starring Michael and his gang, everyday after school at Frederick Douglas Academy High. The only thing missing were the popcorn and comfortable seats. There had been many victims and none stood a chance against Michael and his gang. In this street saga, the bad guy always won. But things were about to change, a new star was about to be born and his name was Kwame. "What you gonna do now, punk!" Michael yelled again as he reached in to shove Kwame in the face this time. However, like a scene in "The Matrix," Kwame did a split to the ground and with his fist tightened, he forcefully delivered a blow to Michael's groin, spun around like a break-dancer, and kicked five of his cohorts in the knees simultaneously, sending them falling face first to the ground. Each received a kick to the groin and flinched in pain while the others cleared the path for Kwame to walk away from the crowd unscathed. There was no point of trying to stand up to a guy who had just dropped five members of their crew with one move. Applause could be heard for blocks as Kwame rushed home hoping that he bought himself enough time from those knuckleheads to make it home safely, one more time.

Kwame had changed the odds in his favor and he didn't even stick around for the glory that most kids would want to bask in. He was a simple man and a loner who had no fear and didn't allow people to push him around. The embarrassment Michael suffered in front of the whole school forced him and his gang to leave Frederick Douglas Academy High School and set up shop somewhere else at a high school in Manhattan. The weird kid finally had a name and from that day on, everybody referred to him as Kwame. He had gotten rid of a bully that had tormented students at the school for months. Even the teachers were afraid of Michael, because he had slashed a few tires and broken a few windshields when he didn't get the kind of grades he felt he deserved without doing any work, whatsoever. It was good riddance and everybody could go back to learning again. The rest of Kwame's junior year went by without any problems.

Kwame was pretty much consumed by karate during his summer break. He would work his part-time job as a camp counselor at a local camp for kids in Brooklyn, and after work he would head straight to the dojo until closing. He worked relentlessly on developing new techniques that he could personally put to practice in case he had to defend himself. Kwame was even allowed to teach a beginner's self-defense class at the camp. And his students were very excited about his methodical approach to teaching. Kwame was often tested, but never defeated. One night while riding the train home to Brownsville, a group of thugs tried to rob him of his paycheck. It was a Friday evening and most thugs understand clearly that it's pay day for most kids who work a summer job. Not wanting to put in the work to earn their own keep, they were trying to get an easy score.

Kwame appeared to be the perfect victim. While at the booth trying to buy a token for the train, he pulled out the $150.00 stack that he had just gotten from cashing his check, while looking for a small bill to hand to the token clerk. He wasn't paying attention to the four thugs waiting in the wing, watching him, to make a victim out of him. After purchasing his token and making his way through the turnstile, the four thugs jumped the turnstile and began to follow him. He could feel the shadows lurking behind him like a suspenseful scene from a Bruce Lee movie. The token clerk tried calling out the four bandits who didn't pay their way into the train station, but they vanished down to the platform. As Kwame stood waiting for the train, there wasn't another soul in sight. The four bandits split in two groups. After checking their surroundings and making sure that there were no witnesses or undercover police officers around, they decided to make their move. With their knives in hands, two of them approached Kwame and demanded his money, "Look, chump, we can make this the hard way or the easy way. Kick in your dough!" said one of the thugs. "I don't have any money for you," he told them. "Listen, chump, if you don't give up the dough, you're gonna end up in a body bag," said one of the thugs as he flung his knife towards Kwame's stomach while the other one looked on. No other word was said as Kwame noticed the other two thugs a few feet away. It was a battle that was going to be determined by beating the thugs two at a time. Kwame knew that he wouldn't stand a chance against four men armed with knives. So, before the other two thugs could get any closer, he acted like he was going into his pocket to hand over the money. While one hand went into his pocket, the other hand went behind his back and a pair of nunchucks came out swinging, hitting the first dude closest to him right in the chin. The unanticipated blow knocked him down to the ground. A left kick met the other thug's lips, and he fell back while his knife dropped out of his hand down on the train tracks. The other two thugs moved in, swinging their knives like they were part of the cast of *Westside Story*. Kwame took notice of their inability to handle a knife. He set the first one up with a left hook, but as he stepped back to avoid contact, Kwame's right foot found his jaw. Down to the ground he went. Kwame was the hood version of Jean Claude Van Dam. He could kick an egg with his foot with exact precision. By then, one of the other thugs had gotten up and another one was still standing with a knife in hand. Fear took over the eyes of the last standing potential robber, and Kwame could smell it. Finishing off the thugs would be the right thing to do, but Kwame was willing to forgive their mistake. Swinging the nunchucks from right hand to left hand demonstrated Kwame's ability and efficiency in using them, and that kept the thugs at bay. Confusion set in and they had no idea how to defend against "the hood Bruce Lee." Kwame increased the speed of the nunchucks and trepidation was at the highest level on the thugs' faces. Pow! The end of the nunchuck hit the thug who thought he had some heart left on top of his head, while he swung the knife around. He was delusional, and the other one took off running. Kwame stood by and waited for the train to pull to a stop in front of him. By the time he boarded the train, all three thugs were getting back on their feet and making the right decision to leave Kwame alone, but not before Kwame simply flicked his finger like Dikembe Mutombo saying "no, no, no," and smiled as the train pulled away.

Kwame was a man of multi layers. Besides the martial arts, he was also a passionate artist who dedicated some of his time developing many comic strip heroes. He sort of lived through those heroes he created for his comic books. His imagination took him places where his main concern was always about making his neighborhood a safer and better place for all those who lived there. Robin Good was one of his favorite characters. Robin Good was a boy who basically robbed the drug dealers and gave the money to shelters and other organizations to help the poor. He had no special training except for his exceptional gift of gab and the ability to get through small places. Robin Good could rob the president while charming the pants off him. He was very charismatic and knew how to turn on the charm to get even the most evil person to trust him. Kwame also developed a character named Mean Hakeem. Mean Hakeem was a character designed to fight injustice, police brutality and rogue cops. He was a well-trained martial artist with the military expertise to destroy a whole army by himself. Mean Hakeem was also a motivator and a brave man. Mean Hakeem believed in fighting for what's right and the betterment of his people in the hood. And the last character was Brainiac, his favorite. Brainiac was a character developed to be a problem solver. He was a crime fighter who believed in using psychological approaches to solve crimes in the hood. Brainiac could basically set up people and make them appear guilty even when they're not. His psychological tactics gave him an edge because he could root out evil, liars and bad people very easily.

Kwame also enjoyed spending time with his little sister who was his only friend. While his mother went to work, he took his sister to the dojo with him and tried his best to keep her close to him all the time. In the summer time, she would go away to camp and that was the only time they were apart. Kwame loved his mother dearly and there was nothing in the world that he would not do for her, and his sister. He was reared with integrity from the time he was born. He never accepted gifts from strangers and always felt comfortable in his skin. Even though his family didn't have much, Kwame was always proud.

Leaving The Nest

It took all of Ms. Janice Robinson's efforts and energy to keep her son from becoming a statistic. She did the best she could to instill values and integrity in her children. However, raising a boy sometimes proved challenging for Ms. Robinson. She couldn't understand why NYPD officers constantly harassed her son for no reason while he walked home from school. She grew suspicious of him at times, because she truly believed that the cops would not go to such lengths without Kwame giving them reasons to do it. Most of the time, Kwame kept the harassment to himself because he knew that his mother wouldn't understand. It was hard to teach his mother about a lesson learned by a black boy. Only another black man would understand how catastrophic it could be for a young black man without a moment's notice. Kwame was tired of reading about the NYPD's inappropriate handling of situations involving black men. New York City was fast becoming a hunting ground for young black men at the hands of the NYPD and Kwame took notice. Absurd drug laws such as, The Rockefeller Drug laws passed by the state legislature, were sending young black men upstate to serve life sentences by the thousands.

Kwame also realized that not everyone that the NYPD labeled a drug dealer were actually drug dealers. Many young black men did fall victim to the trappings of drugs, and the NYPD's overzealous drive to incarcerate them was at an all-time high. The aggressive approach that New York City's mayor, Rudy Giuliani, and the police commissioner took in order to rid New York City's neighborhoods of drug dealers, jeopardized the civil liberties of all black men. The stop and frisk laws enacted were designed to give the NYPD a free pass to harass young black men, and those laws were often abused because NYPD officers knew that they could get away with violating the rights of law abiding citizens. "The shoot 'em first and ask questions later," mentality caused many young black men to be buried unjustly, leaving behind grieving mothers and litigation against the city that cost the taxpayers millions of dollars in settlement fees. The chaotic state of the city was enough to drive a sane man crazy, but even worse, if that man was black. It was time to get outta dodge for Kwame.

Kwame saw his position and realized that he had to come up with a plan to play with the cards that he was dealt. Sting operations were rampant in his neighborhood and the Brownsville projects had become breeding grounds for drug dealers. The future was bleak and Kwame was looking for the light. If only he could join the NYPD right after high school, maybe he could make a difference in his neighborhood and community, he thought. However, that wish vanished because of age eligibility and other detractors and factors that would keep him from getting accepted into the force. For one thing, Kwame despised dirty cops. And secondly, he wanted to rid his community of the bad apples without taking flight to the suburbs. He wanted to stay in his community to make a difference. All that added up to the impossible. Being the realist that he is, Kwame decided a sabbatical from Brooklyn was in his best interest.

Watching the evening news every night also helped influence his decision to leave Brooklyn to pursue his dreams in the United States Armed Forces. The over-saturation of young black men being led in handcuffs as if all black men were criminals; the over-exposure of addicts in the neighborhood rummaging through trash cans looking for something to eat as if they were animals; the constant mention of robberies and other crimes being committed by young black men were enough to have the world believe that all black people are evil. To a certain degree, it worked. Kwame recognized that black men are feared by mostly every group that inhabits the States. Whether it's the newly arrived immigrant from India, China and even Africa, they are all taught to fear the African-American male. White people have always made it clear to society that the black man is to be feared for his criminal nature. However, in the grand scheme of things, the real criminals and the real thieves are white people, Kwame learned. While reading his history books, Kwame also gained the knowledge that most of the world's resources have been stolen by the white man, whether it was in Africa, the Middle East, South America or the Caribbean. The continent with the most natural and richest resources is Africa, but most Africans live in squalor because those resources have been stolen from them by Europeans who colonized most of the continent. Kwame was just starting to understand how the media worked to manipulate one group of people against the rest of the world, and he didn't like it. Though it was hard to grasp the reality of leaving his mother and sister in a desolate, hopeless place on their own, Kwame knew that he would return a better person in order to improve their situation. He was dedicated to giving his family a better life and helping to make his community better. Kwame was all set for the challenge ahead.

Kwame's Research

Kwame tried his best to educate himself through research before signing up for the Navy SEALs. He talked to other officers and went to the library to learn about the mission and history of the Navy SEAL. He didn't want the Navy to educate him; instead, he educated himself before even attempting to join them. As a young man, Kwame was a history buff and researcher who spent most of his time at the library researching everything that he wanted to know and learn. The dojo was his first home and the library was a close second. However, more importantly, Kwame wanted to know how he could utilize his learned skills in the Navy to benefit the work he planned on doing after his honorable discharge. At first, becoming a superhero of some sort for the hood was not at the forefront of his mind, but as his research lingered, he discovered that many of the skills they offered to a Navy SEAL could actually help set into gear his missions for when he returned home.

Through his research, Kwame found out that the Navy SEAL's origin could be traced as far back to the Scouts and the Raiders of World War II. They were early unconventional warfare teams that rival today's

Naval Special Warfare warriors. He was fascinated with the idea of the SEALs, but more importantly, he was impressed with the fact that President John F. Kennedy was the one who called for the creation of the Navy SEALs in order to have a new force with the ability to perform clandestine operations in maritime and riverine environments. The US Navy established SEAL (Sea, Air, Land) Teams One and Two to answer the call. However, things would change in the near future when SEALs would take the lead on virtually every military action. SEALs have carried out 75 special reconnaissance and direct action missions against terrorists trying to escape by sea; SEALs played a significant role in Operation Iraqi Freedom during the early '90's; they also fought in the war against terrorism in the Philippines and the Horn of Africa. But Kwame was most impressed by their ability to use electronic warfare, computer network operations, psychological operations, and military deception to influence, disrupt, corrupt or usurp oppositions' decision-making while protecting Americans. Joining the SEALs also offered Kwame the opportunity to see the world. He had been confined to Brooklyn all of his life, he often wondered what the rest of the world was like.

There were many other aspects of the SEALs that attracted Kwame. The psychological component of the training of the SEALs would help Kwame understand further the underlying problems facing his community. The passing of information to the opposition to influence their emotions, motives, reasoning and ultimate behavior would help Kwame in his future dealings and interaction with people, authority and foes. The training in direct action missions would enable Kwame the ability to seize information, capture, or destroy designated personnel, enemies or material. His training in foreign affairs would help him deal with the bad cops as enemies and aggressors in his community. Most of the training was appealing to a fearless Kwame. He was a just guy who wanted to do his part in society. As he continued to learn new things about the Navy SEALs, he became more excited about the possibilities. The Special Reconnaissance missions would train him to familiarize himself with the enemy's territory. He would not be caught off guard or unprepared for any possible future mission. Special tactical training in Unconventional Warfare (UW), a.k.a. guerilla warfare, employed by Special Forces to equip, advise and assist forces in enemy-held or controlled territory was very attractive. Kwame would also receive Basic Underwater Demolition/SEAL Training, Basic Parachute Training and advanced training. He knew overall his Navy SEAL training would prepare him for any combat environment. In addition, he was happy that he would be able to assist his mother financially because SEALs receive military pay and allowances, plus $375.00 a month dive pay, $300.00 a month Special Delivery

Vehicle (SDV)pay, $225.00 a month HALO (jump) pay and $110.00 a month special duty assignment pay and various amounts per month for second-language proficiency. Considering he would not have to worry about room and board, the opportunity was hard to pass up. Kwame was on his way to signing up for the Navy SEALs.

A Seal In The Making

It was during his senior year in high school that Kwame started contemplating his plans for the future. While many things were milling around in his head, he wanted to challenge himself physically as well as intellectually. Kwame was only seventeen years old when he entered his senior year in high school. It was hard for him to get inspiration from any of the people around his neighborhood, as most of them were doing nothing and being nothing. Kwame didn't want to end up like most of them. Having grown up in the Brownsville section of Brooklyn, Kwame saw poverty and struggle firsthand. His mother worked hard to finally earn her Bachelor's Degree in Elementary education while trying to take care of two kids. Even after she received her degree, it was still hard to make ends meet. Most teachers in New York live on the cusp of poverty, depending on the size of their family and what part of town they reside in. Kwame's mother didn't earn enough to move to Park Slope or Clinton Hill, so she was stuck in the ghettos of Brownsville with her two children, living in close proximity to the Brownsville projects.

After graduating from high school, Kwame wasted no time meeting with a recruiter from the US Armed Forces. He researched every branch of the military before settling on the Navy. His high proficiency in reading, writing, speaking and understanding of the English language gave him an advantage when he decided to take the ASVAB, which is the entrance exam for all the branches of the military. His birthright as a US citizen qualified him for any branch of the US Armed Forces. Since Kwame was never a juvenile delinquent, he had a clean record with no misdemeanor or felony history. He had perfect 20/20 vision and looked like he was in good physical shape due to his martial arts training. Kwame was a well-qualified candidate and the Navy was happy to have him as part of their low minority pool of recruits.

Kwame had been a gym rat since he started taking martial arts lessons when he was a kid. His stamina was unbelievable. The Navy Special Operations Motivator was in awe while he administered the PST for Kwame. No one in the past had ever made the physical training look so easy. Kwame was a physical beast dedicated to his fitness, but more importantly, he sought the intellectual fitness to match the physical. The Navy had made it clear to him that SEAL training is extremely demanding and is not designed to get him in shape. When the physical regimen was outlined for him, Kwame went to work, so he could exceed all the requirements. The basic requirements were like a mini triathlon: 500 yards of swimming, using breast or sidestroke in less than 12 minutes and 30 seconds; 42 push-ups in 2 minutes and 2 minutes rest, 50 sit-ups in 2 minutes and 2 minutes rest; 6 pull-ups; 1.5 miles run in less than 11 minutes in boots and long pants. It was a very demanding regimen and Kwame completed it with flying colors. After boot camp, Kwame was informed that he made the cut to move on to a two-week apprenticeship Training Division School with immediate assignment to (BUDS) Basic Underwater Demolition SEAL training. The Navy SEAL training not only stretched him beyond his limits, but it also made him feel worthy enough to serve with the world's best fighting force. Kwame was prepared to make mature choices, keep his focus and attempt to understand the world around him.

Joining the SEALs was the best option for Kwame because of his vast interests. He was interested in unconventional warfare, direct action, counter drug operation and a host of other things that were presented to him. He was lucky enough to get assigned on his first mission to unconventional warfare in Iraq. It was there that Kwame developed his survival skills while fighting the Jihad militants and the Taliban. He spent a total of three years in Iraq and Afghanistan fighting guerilla wars with Bin Laden's fateful. In Afghanistan, he was able to put to use his learned skills in counter-drug operations and personnel search and recovery, and he also saw direct action in Iraq while using unconventional warfare tactics.

Kwame became a distinguished SEAL. His stealth and clandestine methods of operation allowed him to be a part of several missions against targets that officers from other branches of the military couldn't. The intelligence he gathered in the field helped provide his commanders immediate and virtually unlimited options in the middle of a quandary in Iraq and Afghanistan.

Jackie Robinson

Jackie had been in a state of paranoia due to the heightened feeling she received from the never ending crack sessions. Jackie was once one of the most beautiful girls in the Brownsville area. Her beautiful, medium dark complexion, straight white teeth, almond eyes and bob hairstyle coupled with her perfect size six curvaceous body, made her the target of every young man coming up in Brownsville and the envy of every young lady. Though only a sixteen year-old when her brother left to join the military, Jackie looked like she was a grown woman. When Kwame was home, none of the young men dared coming to the house to bother Jackie. Kwame was quick to put an ass-whipping on any of the young men who tried to get with his sister. Feared by most because of his martial arts ability, Kwame usually didn't have to say much to get his point across.

Meanwhile, Jackie was developing as a young woman and there was no way that Kwame could keep her from dating. After Kwame left, Jackie found herself lonely most of the time because she didn't have any friends. At school, she barely talked to anybody because she was so close to her brother. Kwame was on a mission to keep his sister from becoming a statistic. After Kwame graduated from Brownsville Academy High School, he left behind a vulnerable woman and a socially awkward beauty queen to adjust all on her own. His sister had a hard time adjusting because her protector and best friend was gone. She became an easy target for all those people who were enemies of her brother and the ones who wanted a piece of her. It was hard. Jackie would often go home and complain to her mother about her situation, but her mother saw it as nothing more than growing pains for a teenager. When her grades started slipping, that's when her mom decided to take a proactive approach to help her, but it was a little too late. By then, Jackie had befriended the wrong crowd and smoking weed every day had become habitual and a stress reliever for her.

Jackie started hanging around with the popular kids and they took advantage of her. Since she was one of the prettiest girls in the school, Jackie easily became a pawn in the game of playing guys for their money. She didn't benefit much from the game, but her girlfriends were all benefactors of it. It wasn't long until Jackie started talking to Little Rob, the biggest weed dealer at the high school. Her girlfriends were trying to find a way to get free weed every day, and Little Rob had an endless supply. Out of the whole crew, Little Rob seemed to be infatuated only with Jackie. The other girls in Jackie's circle were throwing themselves at him, but he only had eyes for Jackie.

Rumor had it that Little Rob wasn't just getting paid, but he was also packing some serious beef. While her friends were interested in the amount of beef Little Rob was packing, Jackie saw him as nothing more than a joint supplier for her crew. Little Rob played along and gave Jackie enough weed for her and her crew whenever the girls talked Jackie into asking him for weed.

Since the weed was free, the need to get high increased over time. Jackie tried her best to keep her new addiction from her mother by covering the strong scent of weed with the latest perfume she started buying with the money she was making from her part-time job as a cashier at the local supermarket. She was slowly becoming the social butterfly and her mother didn't see anything wrong with it. She even had a slumber party at her house once with her newfound friends. The girls were always friendly and respectable and Janice didn't see any harm in her daughter having friends. At sixteen years old, Jackie wanted to party with her friends as well. Coincidentally, most of her friends lived in the projects and mostly everything they did revolved around the projects. It wasn't long before Jackie was invited to a party in one of the buildings in the projects and she showed up looking a lot different than her classmates were used to. Her overly tight jeans, high heel boots, halter top, and the flawless make up she wore made her look like she belonged on the cover of *Teen magazine*. She was gorgeous and everybody took notice. Jackie was the talk of the party and her girlfriends were happy to be associated with her. It was the first time she laid eyes on the ruggedly handsome running-back from the football team, away from school, she thought was so cute. She caught his attention as well. After more eye contact, the two ended up dancing the night away together. She was giddy when she got home later that night, because she had so much fun. However, she did notice that Little Rob was soaking up the attention all the other girls at the party were bestowing upon him. He was the popular drug dealer with the fly clothes, money and a car, but Jackie wasn't impressed.

As time went on, Jackie and the star running-back started going out. He was kind and nice to her, but his focus was the next level in college. He was a senior at the high school. He had already signed a letter of intent to one of the best football programs in the south and he didn't want any distraction. Jackie did however, lose her virginity to him. Little Rob was heated when word got around that Jackie had given it up to the running-back. He gave away all that weed was for no reason at all, he felt. He at least thought she would break him off with oral, but Jackie was not that type of girl. Though she wanted the relationship with her prince to continue, she also understood that he had to focus on his collegiate career and football, which was his ticket out of the projects. They parted on good terms and remained friends.

Even though Little Rob was pissed and it was eating him that another man had the girl he wanted, he didn't let it show. He continued to play the role of supplier and acted like he wasn't sweating the situation. Since half the girls at the school wanted to sleep with Little Rob, anyway, he decided to play it to his strength. He wanted Jackie to want to be his number one. As time went on, Jackie wasn't swayed and Little Rob decided it was time to do something about it. Just like his dead daddy, Black Rob, Little Rob had a sinister streak, and Jackie was about to suffer the consequences.

After Little Rob realized that Jackie wasn't going to willingly let him taste her goods, he decided to use a different approach and humiliate Jackie and her friends in the process. The supply of weed to Jackie and her girls never ended and Little Rob continued to be a man of his words by keeping the flow of weed rolling Jackie's way. However, one of the reasons Jackie was never attracted to Little Rob was because he was known as a male whore. Little Rob had slept with most of the pretty girls at the school and he bragged about it to all of his friends. He couldn't wait to conquer Jackie so he could brag about her forbidden fruit. Jackie stood her ground and also made it clear to Little Rob that if he wanted her to start paying for her weed she had no problem with that. This conversation took place after Little Rob tried to get at Jackie and she shut down his advances. Both sides were on the same page, at least that's what Jackie thought.

It was Friday afternoon when school was about to let out when Jackie and her friends were planning their weekend and the smoking sessions that would take place at one of the girl's house who lived in the projects. Little Rob promised to drop a few joints at the girl's house for them to smoke as usual, and nothing else was said. Four joints were tightly rolled and delivered to the girls. After smoking the joints that evening, the girls kept wanting more and more and couldn't understand why. They called Little Rob and asked him to bring four more joints. "I don't know what kind of weed that was, but you need to bring us back a couple more joints for the night," Jackie told him while she was high as a kite. He could hear the other women giggling in the background. "You know I can't give you all more from my supply without charging you for it. How about I just charge you $10.00 for the next batch?" he reluctantly asked. Jackie relayed the message to the girls and they agreed to pay his fee. About a half hour later, Little Rob made the delivery as promised. Not even a couple of hours after his delivery, the girls wanted more joints again. When he noticed the name on his phone when it rang, he knew his plan had worked. The girls were weightless. It was time for Jackie to put in some work to get her next hit.

Little Rob

Little Rob was the only living son of Black Rob who got shot during a robbery gone wrong seventeen years ago. Though he had 4 other siblings, they were all girls and they all had different mamas. Hustling was in Little Rob's blood and he couldn't shake it off. He was still in middle school and only twelve years old when the older dealers had him on the block selling weed and being a lookout. He worked his way up through the ranks and gained the trust of one of the top dealers in Brownsville Projects. By the time he was fourteen and in high school, he had assembled a team of five guys to help him distribute his weed throughout the neighborhood. He started out buying a pound of weed a week and bagging nickel and dime bags for distribution himself. By the time he was a freshman in high school he had increased his business to five pounds a week and took in a couple of his boys as associates. Little Rob tried as much as he could to keep from being flashy, but he couldn't resist buying an occasional pair of Jordans, designer jeans and other gear. He was on the come-up, but he didn't want popo to find out. He also took on a part-time job at the local athletic store on Rockaway Avenue, down the street from where he lived. He had legitimate employment and he could buy anything he wanted with his paycheck. Everyone knew he worked at the athletic store and most of his weed customers knew where to find him. Little Rob made more money selling weed at that store than he could've ever made earning his paycheck.

The owner of the store was happy to see that Little Rob brought so much traffic to his store. Little did he know that all the traffic didn't benefit his store, but Little Rob's pocket, and the drug empire he was trying to build. Occasionally, a customer or two might buy a pair of sneakers or other items in the store to ward off suspicion. The money was rolling in and Little Rob was happy. At this point, he was going to school only to show off his clothes, so he could sleep with the little fast women. The one time he tried to approach Jackie when she was a freshman in high school, Kwame shut him down and threatened to kick his ass if he came near his sister. Kwame was a junior at the time and he had beaten one of the toughest dudes at the school and everybody feared him. Little Rob knew well enough not to mess with Kwame. He stayed in his lane and never bothered Jackie until after Kwame graduated. Still, Little Rob didn't even have enough credit courses after three years of high school to be labeled a freshman. He was definitely not in school to do any work. Since the state mandated that he attended school until the age of sixteen, the teachers had no choice but to let him in their class, but Little Rob never carried a book bag that had any books in it. The only time he carried a book bag was when he wanted to bring his weed to school to stash it in his locker. It was easier to keep his stash at school because he could keep an eye on it all day. Also, Little Rob had never dealt his drugs with his fellow students until a couple of years later.

In his third year of high school, Little Rob started making more money than he could ever dream of. His click of five guys were averaging almost $10,000 each a week selling weed. Little Rob had cash hanging out his ass and he lived it up with his crew at the ripe young age of seventeen. He bought a 3 series BMW that was a couple of years old, but he had the car tricked out better than a brand new one. He was the envy of every wannabe thug in the projects. He also had his enemies, but Little Rob was not a fighter. He was all about the ladies. His boys handled all his beefs. As long as he kept that money coming, his boys would do anything to protect him. A few months into the third year of high school, everyone in Little Rob's click was driving a 3 series BMW. They became known as the BMW Click. A couple of them were stone cold killers, while others were brawlers. Little Rob lived the life that every up-and-coming young drug dealer dreamed about. He stayed in charge of his crew by keeping his connects away from his crew. They had no choice but to get their supply from Little Rob.

Little Rob's mom wasn't blind to his dealings on the street. Her project apartment was laced out like a penthouse. She used to tell Little Rob old war stories about his father. She made him sound like he was the ultimate hustler. She figured Little Rob was a natural hustler by blood, and reaped the benefits of her son's drug dealing. She had all types of fur coats, designer clothes, handbags, shoes, coats, hats and a BMW of her own, courtesy of her son. However, Little Rob's mom cautioned her son not to deal cocaine because of the amount of time he might serve in case he got caught. Little Rob promised her that he would never go that route, but after one of the members of his crew pointed out to him another crew that was making five times the money they were making while selling crack, greed superseded his promise to his mother. Little Rob was no longer content with his BMW and wanted to change the look of his entire click. It was 7 series time, but used cars would be a thing of the past. Little Rob didn't totally alienate his weed operation, but he was ready for bigger and better things. He decided to reach out to one of his connections for his first cocaine deal. His reputation as a weed dealer preceded him and many people in the cocaine and crack distribution welcomed his presence. After buying his first gram of coke and learning how to turn it to crack, he needed a guinea pig to ensure that he had done it properly. Unfortunately, Jackie and her friends became Little Rob's first customers.

The first time Jackie took a puff of what she thought was a regular joint from Little Rob, she became hooked. In actuality, Little Rob had given Jackie and her friends what's known on the street as a "woolie." The high was so good, strong and quick, she needed another hit right away. A woolie is a joint laced with crack cocaine and smoking it has a direct effect on the nervous system. As Jackie passed the joint around, all the girls felt like they were on cloud nine and it was the kind of high that they didn't want to end. Little Rob had always wanted to get back to Jackie for not hooking up with him, but now she was at his mercy and hooked on crack after the first hit. It didn't take long for Jackie and her friends to realize that crack was the center of their world. They would do anything to get it. Little Rob saw her addiction as a way to humiliate her. It took very little time for him to start demanding blowjobs and other sexual favors from Jackie and her friends, because they couldn't afford to pay for their own crack supply. Jackie ended up getting fired from her part time job because half the time she was too high to remember she had a job. She also tried her best to keep her addiction from her mother, but her sticky fingers became a dead giveaway. She stole and sold every little knick knack around her house that she didn't think her mother would miss. As her addiction got worse, she didn't even care that her mother knew that she had stolen the DVD player, TV, stereo and anything of value around the house to support her habit.

Janice Robinson

Meanwhile, Janice Robinson wasn't exactly the exemplary mother either. Janice had started dating this man who was a musician in a local band and the man was all about a good time. Janice had gone to a couple of his shows and he was really a fun guy and she enjoyed being around him. All the hanging out Janice had been doing with her new boyfriend left Jackie unsupervised and to make her own decisions. The musician wasn't just good, he was great. He had Janice in the palm of his hand.

Since Janice never really had a chance to lead the life of a normal teenager, she decided she would start acting like a teenager when she was in her late thirties. Kwame was gone in the military and she had a teenage daughter who was two years away from leaving home to go to college. Jackie figured it was time for her to start living life. Other than Jack, Janice didn't really have sex with any other men. Well, counting the two men she allowed to perform oral sex on her on two different occasions, her sexual experience was limited. When Janice met Chauncy, she fell for him right away. He wasn't the typical man around the way that she was used to seeing all the time. He was a downtown man with a talent that drove people crazy. Chauncy was the saxophonist and maestro of his own jazz quintet called Chauncy and the Horns, and they packed the house every night at the Blue Note in the village. People lined up to come see Chauncy and his band rock the house.

Maybe it was fate on that particular day, but Janice had always turned down her coworkers' invitation to hang out with them at the jazz club after school. For some reason when two other teachers, whom she considered associates, invited her to meet at the Blue Note later that evening, she agreed to go. The house was packed that night. Chauncy and his band were ready to jam. When Janice first laid eyes on him, all she could think about was Bleek, from "Mo Better Blues," the character played by Denzel Washington. Chauncy was tall, dark and handsome and was wearing the hell out of this three button black suit, white collared shirt, black shoes and black sunglasses. Chauncy's sexy physique could be seen through his biceps as he lifted his hands to handle his saxophone like she was his woman. After introducing the band while caressing his instrument and allowing the ladies to hear his smooth baritone, he took to the stage for an interpretation of Sade's "Smooth Operator." The smooth sound of Chauncy's saxophone had the ladies melting in his hands while their panties moistened. Janice was all smiles while she replayed different scenes from her favorite movie as Chauncy took the lead role, in her head. Janice wasn't the only one doing the admiring. Behind the dark shades, Chauncy couldn't keep his eyes off the pretty black woman sitting in the front with two other women. His performance was a little extra that evening because he wanted to make an impression on Janice. By intermission, Chauncy could no longer stand back and watch Janice. He had to say something to her. Janice wasn't looking to shabby herself. Her co-workers were a little surprised that Janice had shown up at the club wearing a sexy little black dress that revealed all the curves that God had blessed her with, and the sexiest pair of legs that they had ever seen. Her dress barely sat above her knees and it gave the illusion that her thighs were the pathway to heaven. Her co-workers had only seen the conservative Janice at work wearing pantsuits, most of the time. They were a little envious of her curves and body.

Chauncy didn't want to be too obvious, so after he got off the stage, he walked straight to the bar and asked the waitress to deliver a drink to Janice on his behalf. Janice was all smiles when the waitress pointed towards Chauncy at the bar to identify him as the culprit behind the delivered drink. Grand Marnier on the rocks looked very sexy on Janice's lips. He also sent a personal message for Janice to wait for him after he's done with his next set via the waitress. The other two women sitting at the table with Janice were a little jealous, but they knew it was Janice's time to shine. She was the chosen one of the three women. Suddenly, when Chauncy got back on stage to finish his set, he didn't look so sexy to the other two women anymore, because he had his heart set on Janice. The sudden urge to leave the club was an obvious sign of jealousy by the two women, but Janice decided to stay because she wanted to see what Chauncy was all about. "Well girlfriend, you know we gotta be up early for school in the morning, we're gonna check you out tomorrow," one of the ladies said as the other looked on. "You realize today is Friday, right?" Janice reminded them. "It is, isn't it? Well, we still have to go because we have things to do in the morning," she retorted with a laissez faire attitude. There was a reason why Janice never had any female friends; she never got along with them. Even the ones she considered associates seemed to have a problem with her. Janice was not snooty, uppity or bourgie, she was as down to earth as they come. She came from a humble background and she never once tried to forget it. Those two women had just downgraded their status to simple coworkers. They were no longer acquaintances or associates of Janice. She knew exactly how to deal with them from then on.

After the ladies left, Chauncy decided to dedicate a special song that he wrote to Janice called, Special Lady. It was one of the smoothest grooves that the band had played all night. Janice was all flustered because she was not used to so much attention. However, she also felt very special. Once the set was over, Chauncy came over to her table and took care of her tab before they left the club together. "Since the weather is so nice, how about we take a walk around the village?" he suggested. "That sounds good, but do you invite every woman that comes to the club to take a walk with you?" she asked curiously. "I'm not gonna lie to you, I have, but only the special ones," he said while flashing his pearly whites to her. It was the first time that Janice had gotten a chance to see Chauncy's perfect smile up close. "You know it's hard to read somebody's eyes while they're wearing shades. How about you allow me to read your honesty through your eyes?" she politely asked. Chauncy had forgotten that he was no longer on stage, and out of force of habit, kept his glasses on. He quickly pulled them off to expose the sexiest light brown eyes that Janice had ever seen on a man his complexion, but they were a little glazed, like he hadn't gotten enough sleep. She figured he was wearing those glasses for a reason after he took them off.

Janice and Chauncy continued to walk down Sixth Avenue towards uptown while they shared great conversation. She was a little surprised when he invited her to his apartment located not too far away in Chelsea. "That's a little forward, don't you think?" she said to him after the invitation to his place. "Well, it all depends on how you look at it. Maybe I don't want to share my special moment with you and the rest of the bustling crowd in New York City. Perhaps, I'm selfish and I want my alone time with you," he said jokingly.

Janice figured Chauncy was a little different because he was a musician and he didn't like to be in public so much because he was always on display while performing. "If I agree, to go to your place, do you promise not to take advantage of my decision?" she asked in a serious tone. "Only if you promise to do the same," he repeated while holding her hands. Janice felt comfortable enough with the Bleek lookalike to go to his place. He hailed a cab that took them a few blocks up the street to Chelsea.

Chauncy

Right away Janice was impressed when she set foot into Chauncy's apartment. She had never been inside a Manhattan loft before. The structure of the place and the contemporary designs left her flabbergasted. The two story apartment with 9ft ceilings was very inviting. Upon entering the apartment, she noticed the bright colored hardwood floor and the exposed bricks on the wall as she made her way to the spacious living room. The kitchen and dining room hid behind the wall in the hallway. It was the first time she had seen high-end stainless appliances outfitted in a kitchen so nice that she felt like cooking for Chauncy. The tan marble countertop in the kitchen matched perfectly with the marble tile backsplash along the wall behind the sink and the rest of the countertop. The mahogany cabinets with glass doors were set so beautifully, she felt the need to open and close them to see what kind of china Chauncy had hidden in there. There were quite a few beautiful imported pieces that moved her. Moving to the dining room, she noticed the contemporary Italian designed iron table with a glass top and chairs that appropriately sat in the middle of the room under what seems to be a contemporary light, decorated as a chandelier. While she admired his place, he offered to take her jacket to hang it up in the closet. She moved to the bright living room where she sat on the yellow leather couch, at the urging of Chauncy. The couch was designed in what seemed to be an L shape that she had never seen before. There was a bright red leather chair, a glass table and a multicolored Persian rug underneath the coffee table in the middle of the room. There was a fireplace across from the couch and an entertainment center with a television consul as well as a stereo. The walls were outfitted with original as well as contemporary life-size framed replicas of famous artworks by Jean Michel Basquiat, Jacob Lawrence, William H. Johnson, Augusta Savage, and other well known African American artists. Though the apartment was colorful, everything seemed fluid throughout. Chauncy obviously was a man of taste, she thought. She felt he was in a different league; a league that she didn't think existed. Janice couldn't believe her eyes. She guessed that Chauncy was probably doing pretty well for himself.

A few minutes after Janice sat down, Chauncy took off his jacket, and walked over to Janice, "Would like something to drink?" he asked as he pointed to the mini bar in the right corner of the living room. "I think I've had enough drinks for the night. Can I please have some water?" Janice requested. "Sure. Whatever the lady likes," he said with enthusiasm. He went into his subzero fridge and pulled out a bottle of Evian water. "Would you like your water in a glass, hon?" he asked.

"Sure," she answered. Chauncy brought the closed bottle of water along with a clean glass for Janice. He opened the bottle in front of her and proceeded to fill her glass with it. She stopped him about halfway through the glass, suggesting it would be enough. Chauncy moved towards the mini bar to pour himself a shot of Chivas scotch in a glass. Afterwards, Chauncy turned on his stereo to a CD of Norman Brown that was on cue as the two of them conversed on the couch. The conversation flowed so well, Janice didn't even realize how late it had gotten. Chauncy certainly didn't want her to catch the train at 3:00 AM, so he decided to offer to pay for her cab fare home. "You know I live in Brooklyn, right?" she said to him with a look of uncertainty. "What does that mean, I can't afford to pay for your cab ride home?" he said jokingly. "Don't worry about it. I'm good for it and your time with me was worth every dime," he told her while trying to plant a kiss on her cheek. "Well, I guess that's it. I hope that we can do this again real soon. I really enjoyed your company," Janice assured him. "Well, how about we do it sooner than later? I would love to take you out to dinner tomorrow before my gig," he offered. "I have to check my schedule, but that sounds good," she said flirtatiously. "Oh, we got a schedule now. Well, please tell your people to get in touch with my people, so we can be folks together," he said trying to get her to crack a smile again.

Chauncy really would have preferred for Janice to stay the night with him, but he didn't want to be disrespectful by asking her to stay. Things were going too well between them for him to make the wrong move or say the wrong thing. Quite honestly, Janice contemplated staying the night with him as well, only if he had asked her. She felt like she had known this man forever. She had never been so comfortable with anyone so quickly. Janice and Chauncy talked about their upbringing and the hardship they faced as children. He moved to New York from Chicago to pursue his music and never looked back. Chauncy also studied music at the prestigious Berkeley College of Music in Boston, Massachusetts. When he first started playing professionally, he had an R&B group in Boston that used to play at the local clubs, but his career wasn't going anywhere. After he graduated from Berkeley, Chauncy moved back to Chicago only to be faced with the same reality he faced in Boston. Meanwhile, his interest in jazz was growing by the day. By the time he decided to move to New York to pursue his music full-time, he had decided to focus on Jazz. However, Chauncy had also produced a couple of top ten hits for one of the hottest R&B artists in the country at the time. It was the proceeds from those records that he used to buy his loft. At one point in his life, he was one of the most sought-after producers in the business, but with success came the bitter side of the business. Chauncy bowed out before he got swallowed by the industry. He decided to put together his jazz band a few years back and he has had steady gigs around New York paying them top dollars ever since. Chauncy was financially secure and was trying to enjoy life. He didn't seem to be a complicated man, but Janice was shocked when he revealed some of the platinum hits that he had produced. Some of them were her favorite songs. Like Janice, Chauncy didn't grow up with his dad, and his mother struggled to make ends meet. He was barely five years old when his father was shot by an assassin's bullet looking for a quick score. Chauncy confessed that he had been assisting his mom financially ever since he started working and earning a paycheck. When he received his huge payday for the two top-ten records he penned and produced, he bought his mother a house in a small suburb of Chicago.

Chauncy didn't have any children or family in New York City, but he couldn't wait to meet that special woman to make him whole. On paper, Chauncy was just too perfect. He was the man that many women out there was looking for; financially stable, educated, talented, funny, kind-hearted and good looking. Janice thought she hit the lottery. She didn't believe she could land such a great man. Chauncy also thought that Janice was a catch. She was a single mother working hard to advance herself while raising two children by herself. He was impressed, to say the least.

As Janice got up to put on her so coat she could walk out the door, Chauncy pulled her close for a kiss. The minty Spearmint gum he was chewing abated the alcoholic smell of the scotch he had been drinking. She imagined his lips were soft most of the night, but she was pleasantly surprised when she finally got to play tug of war with his lips while they kissed. He had the softest lips that she had ever kissed. She was so enthralled by it she ended up staying an extra half hour just making out with Chauncy on the couch. After a while, she realized she was treading dangerous water as her needs were about to supersede her wants. Her pussy was throbbing as Chauncy's tongue caressed hers and his hands fondling her back, arms and ass. Janice hadn't gotten so moist in a while and her body was calling him. She decided it was best to go home, because she knew if she spent the night Chauncy would've been all up in her. She wanted it. It was hard for them to break apart from each other, but they eventually did and Chauncy walked her downstairs to put her in a cab. He handed a hundred dollar bill to the impatient cab driver after giving Janice one last kiss. Janice got in the cab and turned around to look at Chauncy in the distance until he disappeared from sight. All she could think about on the way home was how she was gonna make love to Chauncy. He definitely left an impression on her.

Janice and Jackie

Janice never thought much of Jackie's occasional defiant behavior. She attributed her behavior to the growing pains of a teenager. The two of them started butting heads over little things like curfew and Jackie's grades at school. Janice was never suspicious of her daughter's casual drug habit, because Jackie did a good job hiding it from her mother. Usually Jackie would run straight to the bathroom to take a shower and brush her teeth when she got home to keep the smell of marijuana on her body from her mom. Janice was also trying her best to allow Jackie the privacy and the space she needed as a young lady, but occasionally, they would have disagreements. It was hard for Janice to play the role of mother in Jackie's life as Jackie got older, because she had always been more of a friend. The nineteen year difference between them and the fact that Jackie was overly developed for her age made it difficult for Janice to be a stern parent.

Since the departure of Kwame, Janice tried her best to be close to her daughter, and in the process, she eliminated any kind of parent/child boundary that was established. She was even enamored by the fact that people, most of the time, assumed that she was Jackie's older sister. After meeting Chauncy, Janice did all that she could to keep a younger spirit about her and slacked off a little on Jackie. All of a sudden if Jackie didn't come home by her eleven o'clock curfew, she didn't make a big deal of it. Also, because Jackie had decided she would start contributing financially to the household, her mom became more lenient. After Jackie started working her part-time job, she offered to pay the electric, phone as well as the cable bill every month, and her mother was more than grateful. However, the financial responsibility bestowed upon Jackie also came with great freedom. Jackie now felt she could do whatever she wanted because of her contribution to the household. While Janice saw it as fair to allow her daughter a little more freedom than ever before, she also knew that she had to play the role of parent. Keeping the two balanced, however, became a problem. Janice and Jackie would have yelling matches over things such as: the revealing outfits she wore to school, not doing her chores around the house, slacking off in school, staying home from school too many days because of "sickness," and staying out all night on the weekends. Things were changing for the worst and Janice didn't take the appropriate steps to change them. Janice relied on Kwame to help keep Jackie in line, because the two of them had been close since they were young and Jackie looked up to her brother. Every time Janice talked to Kwame, she would put his sister on the phone so he could talk some sense into her, but his lectures were futile because he was so far away. Jackie would sit on the phone and listen to her brother and promised not to do whatever it was that her mother was complaining about, but a few days later she would go right back to her old ways. Kwame had even threatened to come home a couple of times to talk to her face to face, but he never delivered on his threats.

Meanwhile, Jackie's drug use was escalating to levels that were beyond casual. She and her friends were spending most of their time getting high. Even on her days off at work, Jackie told her mother she was working so she could go hang out with her friends and get high. Her friends didn't help the situation much because their addiction to marijuana was five times stronger than Jackie's. Janice didn't really know what to do. Grounding Jackie was not an option because of she contributed to the household bills. And there was no way she was ever going to physically abuse her daughter. She prayed that God would help in guiding Jackie in the right direction.

Janice in Love

There were other reasons why Janice started to get a little careless with her daughter; she was falling in love with Chauncy. It didn't take long for Janice to fall for Chauncy's charm. After seeing Chauncy a couple more times, Janice couldn't help falling in love with him. She started to experience extravagant dinners, getaway weekends to Atlantic City, Vegas and Miami, great sex and most of all, happiness, whenever Chauncy didn't have a gig. Janice hadn't experienced love and happiness in a long time. The last time she felt this good was when Jack was alive. She and Chauncy were making plans to be together forever. She couldn't wait for Jackie to turn 18 years old, so she didn't have to be responsible for her anymore. She had plans to marry Chauncy and move downtown with him. Janice realized she was in love the first time she shed tears while Chauncy was making love to her.

Chauncy was a nice and easy lover. He caressed Janice's body the same way he caressed his saxophone. It happened one night after they got to his apartment from dinner. Chauncy picked Janice up at the front door and carried her to the bedroom. He tried his best to avoid contact with his forearm while carrying her. She had her arms wrapped around his neck, kissing him all over his face while he whispered sweet lullabies in her ears. "I'm gonna make sweet love to you tonight. You have come into my life and made me the happiest man," he told her. Those words were music to her ears. After placing Janice down on his king size bed, Chauncy proceeded to undress her. It was a little difficult at first to pull off her extra tightly fitted jeans, but with enough wiggling of her legs Chauncy got them below her thighs and down to her ankles, before pulling them off completely with his teeth. Her thick thighs looked delicious and inviting. Feeling a little impatient, Janice pulled off her sweater and lay on her back in her bra and underwear. Her body was exquisite. She had no stretch marks and no overlapping skin to signify she had given birth to two kids. Chauncy stood back and admired Janice's body for a little while before slowly making his way towards her. He slowly started to kiss her shoulders, down to her arms and all the way down to her toes. He definitely had slow hands as they wandered all over Janice's body. The feeling was thrilling to her. She wanted to enjoy the moment. Chauncy was still fully clothed when he started his expedition of Janice's body. The light in the bedroom shined brightly on Janice, revealing her radiant skin and natural beauty that God had created. Chauncy slowly unclasped her bra and proceeded to savor her breasts in his mouth. Her hardened nipples were tasty and her breasts still firm, like a teenager. Chauncy caressed them until Janice became moist beyond control. She held on to his head while he sucked on her breasts. Soon, he made his way up to her lips for a never-ending kiss. The soft smacking of lips and tussling of tongue brought the temperature in the room to boiling hot. Chauncy needed to take off his clothes, but not before dimming the light to a comfortable level of darkness where she could only see his silhouette. The seductive grappling of ass, biceps, triceps, hair and breasts continued for about ten more minutes before Chauncy made his way down to her heavenly canal for a major mind-blowing excursion with his tongue. Janice's pussy was throbbing as Chauncy leisurely rubbed his tongue up and down her clit, while his hands caressed her breasts. Her moaning and groaning was uncontrollable. She tried running her hands down his wavy hair for comfort, but Chauncy was too skilled. Janice started to lose control as she exclaimed, "I'm coming! Oh my god I'm fucking coming!" Chauncy never wavered from her pleas. He continued to satisfy Janice with his tongue until she literally had to pull her body away from his grasp to recollect herself.

Round one was great. Janice had not cum like that before, never! Not even Jack was that skilled orally, she thought. Chauncy was a master at cunnilingus and Janice was almost afraid of his great skill. Now she wondered would he consider her skills good enough to satisfy him. Chauncy was lying on his back with a couple of pillows propped up behind his head when Janice decided to start her own voyage down his pleasure stick. While kneeling over him, she ran her hands up and down his chest before she began to lick his nipples. Chauncy ran his hands through her hair while she left light tracks of her saliva across his chest. He didn't want to hurriedly force her down his crotch, but she got the message when his harden ten-inch dick bumped her across the chest. She reached for it as she made her way down and started slowly stroking it. This was the first time that Janice wasn't shy about taking a dick in her mouth. As a matter of fact, she couldn't wait to taste Chauncy's mandingo. It didn't take much effort for Janice to ease her way down Chauncy's chest to his crotch and placed her mouth on the shaft of his dick while holding the rest in her hand. She slowly sucked and stroked as Chauncy closed his eyes to enjoy her celebrated efforts. The delayed movement of her soft lips around the shaft of Chauncy's dick was pure utopia. There was something different about the way Janice was sucking Chauncy off. It was as if she wanted to make sure he was pleased and not like it was a chore, the way she felt about other men in the past. Though she had only been with a couple of men besides her husband, Janice had put her mouth around a dick or two. However, Chauncy's was the dick she felt she wanted to suck with fervor. The slurping sounds of her tongue as she took his dick in and out of her mouth, only increased his desire to climax. Janice's tongue was magical as Chauncy kept his eyes shut and allowed her to delight him. As he neared climax, he held on to her head tightly and let out a loud moan while she gulped down his protein. Janice had never swallowed a man's cum until then, and she was happy she did it.

Though Chauncy had just released over a teaspoon of semen, his dick remained blood-filled and hardened at the sight of Janice's pear-shaped bottom. From her tiny waist all the way down past her thighs, Janice was a goddess. Chauncy could barely see her silhouette as she lay next to him on her stomach exposing one of God's best creations for man, a nice round booty. He gently smacked her ass as his fingers wandered down to her wetness. He mildly played with her clit using his fingers to maximize stimulation. Janice had never been so wet and horny. Chauncy's finger slid right in and Janice welcomed it. She started grinding on the single middle finger inside her, tempting Chauncy to add his index finger to intensify her pleasure. "I want you to fuck me!" she said almost in a shy way while grinding on Chauncy's two fingers inside her. Chauncy reached into the top drawer on the nightstand and pulled out a golden wrapped Magnum condom. After rolling the condom down his shaft, he pulled Janice towards him with her ass up in the air and her face buried in the pillow. She braced herself for his slow penetration. Her pussy was nice and tight, to Chauncy's delight. He slowly inserted himself inside her while holding on to her beautiful ass. As his dick loosened her pussy up, her mobility increased and she kept backing her ass up on him for a deeper penetration. Realizing that Janice wanted a full course meal and not a snack, Chauncy commenced the pussy adventure. His strokes came from all different angles as he searched for her G-spot. He stood over her and humped up and down while she kept her ass up in the air. She liked every minute of it, screaming, "Fuck me, baby! Fuck me! Your dick is so sweet!" Her dirty talk only fueled his desire to please her. He pulled her off the bed and bent her over on the edge of the mattress to continue fucking her from behind. She could feel all his ten inches inside her as he pounded her pussy with his strongest strokes. Sweet, she thought. As sweat poured down Janice's back, Chauncy bent down to lick it as he continued to fuck her from the back. He held on to her tiny waist and unleashed a series of winds and strokes that sent her to the brink of climax, but he chilled. Recognizing there was more than one way to please a woman, Chauncy decided to opt for a new position. He got on the bed and allowed Janice to ride him. After she got on top of him, his penetration was at a maximum and she could almost feel him hitting her uterus. She slowed down the pace of her movement to magnify the feeling she was experiencing while riding him. While she was enjoying the ride, he played with her clit until she couldn't take it anymore. Tears rolled down Janice's cheeks as she stared straight in Chauncy's face, realizing how great it felt to be with him. Chauncy realized it was the calm before the storm. He increased the speed of his own movements as Janice braced herself for yet another nut. The two of them held on tightly to each other's hand as they both reached an explosive climax that left them comatose for a couple of hours, thereafter. However, before she passed out with her head on his chest, Janice mumbled the three little words he wasn't expecting, "I love you." "Me too," he replied.

Dirty Little Secrets

It had been a while since Janice and Chauncy had been dating. Things were going great and she spent most of her weekends at his place. The two never officially announced that they were an item, but it was understood. Everything appeared to be exclusive between the two of them. Janice was not interested in any other man and Chauncy didn't appear to be interested in other women either. When Janice wasn't busy at work, she was on the phone with Chauncy talking for long hours like their topics of conversation were endless. The more time Janice spent with Chauncy, the deeper her feelings became.

Chauncy made sure Janice understood that their relationship was not a one-way relationship. He was just as much in love with her. It was not unusual for Janice to receive a bouquet of roses at work from Chauncy. Sometimes it was just a card. Chauncy was an expert in the romance department. Janice had never explored Central Park until she met Chauncy. It was while they were taking a stroll at Central Park one day that Chauncy pulled her from the walking trail into the woods to have a quickie with her. Janice had no idea she could be that freaky and voyeuristic. Though the traffic at the park wasn't as usually busy, there was still a decent amount of people walking through the park that spring evening when Chauncy decided to coerce Janice into a quickie. At first, she felt a little too shameful to have sex in public, but by the time Chauncy lifted her dress and had his tongue playing cricket with her clit, she lost control and the only thing she could hold on to was the tree behind her. She could see the people walking by behind bunches of leaves and tree branches, but she held on tight as Chauncy licked her clit like a hungry elephant. She moaned softly as she held on to his head while leaning against the big Royal Paulownia tree. Noticing that Janice was shaking uncontrollably, Chauncy quickly pulled back and got up to kiss Janice. While the two were kissing, Janice started touching him all over, rubbing his flesh like she wanted to be one with him. When Janice ran her hand over his right forearm, he flinched like he was in pain. This was the second time that Chauncy avoided being touched by Janice on his forearm, but the last time was his left forearm. He didn't want it to appear to be a big deal, so he simply held her close to him while he kissed her. Since Janice was already in a naughty mood, she decided to kneel down, pulled Chauncy's dick out through his zipper and she started sucking him off. Chauncy stood back and enjoyed every minute that Janice spent sucking him. When she finally decided to come up for air, he turned her to face the tree while he penetrated her from behind. However, due to the spontaneity of their action, no condom was used.

Chauncy went in raw and he fucked Janice like he was possessed. The warm juices of her pussy around his dick felt like he was in a cocoon. His strokes were rapid and intense. She couldn't help coming over and over again. Chauncy hurried to get one before somebody heard Janice groaning in the woods.

After they were done, the two of them strolled casually on the walking path, hand in hand, like two love birds. While they were walking, Janice went to pull on Chauncy's forearm again, unaware of his earlier complaint, to get him closer to her. He flinched again, but he opted to explain the pain to Janice just to satisfy her curiosity. "Are you ok, baby?" she asked with concern in her voice. He downplayed it by telling her, "I started working out at the gym again this week and my arms are sore. She accepted it as a good probability and dismissed it was anything more than that. She was just happy that someone had finally brought out the freak in her. She left Chauncy that evening feeling renewed, but she also felt like there was something that Chauncy was not telling her. She found it strange that he never wanted to have sex with her in the light, even though he kept telling her how much he admired her body. She noticed that Chauncy had never taken his clothes off until after the lights are dimmed or turned off. He didn't mind seeing her naked in the light, but he always waited until darkness to strip, she thought. The ride back to Brooklyn gave her plenty of time to think about too many things. Janice even started to wonder if her daughter was sexually active. All the random thoughts she was having on the train couldn't take away the twinkle in her eyes and the tingling feeling in her heart for Chauncy.

Chauncy's Skeletons

Chauncy got home that evening, knowing that sooner or later, his skeletons were going to be exposed. He hadn't been to the gym, never! Though his body was cut from doing calisthenics in his house, he wasn't a fan of the gym. His daily routine of three hundred push-ups and two hundred sit-ups gave him the desired body that most women wish for on a man. Chauncy had demons he was dealing with that he couldn't tell Janice about. For the most part he had been a functional addict for the last ten or so years. While on the touring circuit when he was an R&B producer, Chauncy was introduced to heroin by a fellow musician. After taking his first hit from the devilish needle, he couldn't stop. The veins on his forearm were starting to rot because of Chauncy's daily use of heroin. He tried rehab a few times, but it didn't work. He wrestled with the idea of telling Janice about his addiction. He thought she might leave him if he told her the truth. Chauncy had been wrestling with his addiction so long that he learned to cope with it. A shot of heroin infused him with creativity, spontaneity, fervor for life and overall peace of mind and happiness. At least, in his mind that's what the drug provided. The last thing he wanted to be known as was a junkie, which was one of the reasons why he bowed out of the R&B and pop music scene. He knew eventually he would be exposed and he didn't want to disappoint his mother, whom he held dearly in his heart.

Chauncy had been with many women in his life and each one that he met served a purpose for the time they were present in his life. He had never met someone like Janice, whom he felt was genuinely into him just because. He had fun with her and she was easy to be around. Chauncy wasn't always high when Janice was around, but he stayed high most of the time. He wondered if he would ever be able to function without heroin, completely. He even questioned his musical ability without the drugs. Chauncy would never get a chance to find out if he could be musically creative, absent of the drugs in his system, because he couldn't get rid of his demons. The tracks on his arms were the last resort because most of the veins on his legs had already collapsed from years of drug use. In the beginning, Chauncy shot the drugs in his legs to keep his arm clean and to hide his secret from the world. Again, his bruises and marks on his legs were explained away by his rough play as a child. It wasn't hard to sell Janice on his excuses because Janice had never been around a junkie that used a needle to shoot himself with heroin. Crack was the typical drug of choice around her neighborhood, and she could identify a crackhead without a problem. Chauncy wasn't a junkie by choice. He wanted so badly to rid himself of his drug habit, but the drugs had a stronghold on him and the people around him didn't help his situation by shooting up with him. In many cases, most junkies never do drugs alone, as was the case with Chauncy. A good man in every other way, but the worst human vice he could pick up was destroying his life. Chauncy was also at ease when he was high, as heroin was a downer for him. He even contemplated suicide at one point, because he felt he was living a lie. His many stints in rehab proved futile because he would always run into the people that influenced his drug abuse after he left rehab.

Janice's world

Janice felt sad and lonely when the principal called her into his office one day to inform her that she was going to be one of the teachers let go, due to budget cuts by the New York City Department of Education. It was with a heavy heart that the principal had to tell one of his best teachers that he couldn't hold on to her. Janice had transformed her students in a positive way and the principal took notice. She had just started her job as an art teacher two years prior, and was hoping to work on her Master's in education to fulfill the requirements for the Department of Education in order to become a tenured teacher. Chauncy had been a good influence in her life up to that point. He was encouraging and told her she could accomplish anything she wanted. Her evening classes took time away from Chauncy, but the two of them managed to see enough of each other for the last couple of years.

Janice also had to deal with her daughter who was also failing in school. The more Jackie hung out with her friends, the more defiant she became and the more she neglected her school work. Jackie had even started to become delusional to believe that her mother actually loved her brother more than she loved her.

Janice was going through a hard time and praying that she could weather the storm. She knew it was her job to rear Jackie, so she said very little to Kwame about his sister's behavior whenever he called home. She even started to make excuses for Jackie whenever Kwame called and couldn't talk to her. She had Kwame believe that Jackie was busy with work and school, which was the reason she was never home whenever he called. At times, she wished her son was near her, so he could console her and make her feel better. Kwame was Janice's hero. He had only come home once, right after basic training, since joining the Navy. He had chosen to visit other countries whenever he was on leave from the military. Kwame wanted to see the world and he shared his experience with his mother through pictures. Janice was always proud to show pictures of her son from different locations around the world with his friends. That happiness kept Janice together for the most part.

Though Grandma Jones had paid off the house before passing, there remained the annual taxes due every six months and the monthly insurance. After receiving the pink slip from her job, Janice was uncertain as to how she would manage financially. She couldn't place her financial burdens on her daughter, and she definitely didn't want to allow Chauncy to be her savior. She needed to dig herself out and she needed to do it fast. It was hard to find placement in the arts subject for any teacher in any school system, and it was no different for Janice in New York City. The winter semester in January was about to start and Janice needed to line up as many interviews as possible, so she could become gainfully employed. She received a great recommendation letter from her former principal and was hopeful that a position would open up soon. Unfortunately, the cuts went across the board in every school. New York City, a city known for its arts around the world, was cutting the very programs that provided the world with the best artistic talents. Janice hit a brick wall as most of the schools in the New York City public school system was hit with budget restraints due to lack of funding. The arts were affected the most. She resorted to daily substitute gigs to help sustain her life financially. She was also faced with mounting tuition fees from Brooklyn College where she was pursuing her MED (Master's of Education Degree.) Janice's world was collapsing right before her and there was nothing she could do about it. It took a lot of swallowing of her pride to tell her son, Kwame, that she needed his financial assistance. Without a second thought, Kwame agreed to send money home to his mother to help assist with the insurance and the taxes for the house. After all, his grandmother had willed the house to him. Kwame was earning a decent salary in the Navy and he hardly needed to spend his money on anything, as everything was provided for him, except his civilian clothing.

The financial forecast for Janice was a little better, but there was hardly any extra cash. Sometimes she was only able to get work for two days a week and other times none at all. Occasionally, she was able to fill in for a full week when the flu season started to take its effect on teachers, but it was rare. Janice had to become a financial genius in order to make ends meet; every quarter was stretched to a dollar and every penny turned to a miracle quarter. Jackie was eventually fired from her job after showing up to work high. She could no longer contribute and she lied to her mother as to why she was let go. Janice didn't feel the need to pressure her daughter to work, because she felt her daughter was going through her own pain. Jackie felt deserted after her brother left. The struggle continued and Janice made sure she cooked at least enough food everyday to feed herself and her daughter. Life went on.

Keep On Pushing

With her problems mounting, Janice only found solace in the arms of Chauncy. However, Chauncy was trying to navigate his own life with all the demons he had to deal with. Music was his comfort and without music, he would perish. Chauncy was also growing very fond of Janice and he wanted to be there for her if she ever needed him. The two had made plans to spend a getaway weekend together in the Pocono Mountains. Chauncy rented a car and booked a room at one of the most romantic resorts in the Pocono area at Cove Haven Entertainment Resorts in Lakeville, Pennsylvania, considered one of the most romantic resorts in the state. Janice was excited as she packed her clothes to go spend a weekend alone with her man. Chauncy was special. No man had ever taken Janice on a getaway trip before, not even locally. Janice couldn't wait to free her mind and leave behind the stress and miseries of her life for one weekend.

Janice decided to meet Chauncy at his place in Manhattan because it was be easier for him to drive down to the Lincoln Tunnel to catch the turnpike to Pennsylvania. Chauncy was all smiles when Janice showed up wearing a nice pair of jeans, knee high boots, sweater, a knit hat and her Goosedown coat.

Janice was pleasantly caught off-guard by Chauncy's outfit. She had never seen him in Timberlands, jeans and a sweater before. Chauncy shaved about a good twenty years off the forty years he had been living on this earth wearing that outfit. Janice suddenly had a little thug fantasy running through her mind. He was surprised that she packed so light, carrying only one medium sized suitcase for the trip. Janice looked beautiful, wearing simply lip gloss on her lips and no makeup at all. He gave her a quick peck before grabbing her bag and placed it in the trunk of the Jeep Wrangler. The two of them had never spent time together away from New York. This particular weekend was going to be a test for their relationship. Soon after they hit the road, Janice started to allow her curiosity to get the best of her. "What's this place like?" she asked Chauncy. "Well, I think you're gonna be pleasantly surprised. It has all the comforts to make this weekend a weekend full of romance and lovemaking," he said while cracking a wide grin. "Com'on! You're gonna have to do better than that. I want details," she said with anticipation. "Ok, let's just say there's a heart shaped hot tub, enchanting lodging, amorous activities and hopefully endless romance," he teased her. "Ok, I'll let you slide with that for now," she said playfully.

They had been driving for almost forty-five minutes and enjoying a great conversation when Janice revealed, "You know something, Chauncy? I think I'm falling in love with you. I don't just love you anymore; I'm falling in love with you." There was no immediate reaction from Chauncy, but after a long pause he told her, "I fell in love with you the first time I saw you." Those words were enough to draw tears down Janice's cheeks. She reached for his inner thighs to caress them while he drove. "You're in the forbidden area. A brother might crash, feeling this good while driving," he joked. "You call that feeling good? How about if I do this?" she said while unzipping his pants to pull out his snake. Chauncy's hardened penis more than welcomed Janice's touch. She started stroking his dick with her hands gently to get it as hard as Chauncy could possibly get, before she leaned her body over and placed her mouth on it. "How's this for driving you crazy?" she asked while sucking his dick gently. "That right there is driving me crazy nuts. Don't stop. Take me to the cuckoo house." Janice continued to suck until they arrived at their destination, at which time Chauncy decided to allow Janice to finish the job in the parking lot. He came and she swallowed him like an ice cold pi□a colada.

Janice's excitement couldn't be contained as she set foot inside the lobby of the resort. The décor was inviting and romantic. They waited for about ten minutes before they were finally able to check in. Chauncy was excited with key and luggage in hand and Janice in tow as they headed to the room. Upon entering the room, the atmosphere forced them to drop their luggage at the door and become enraptured in unbounded passion immediately. The remnant of what took place in the car was still alive between them, and now it was time to go all the way for round two. Chauncy and Janice were covered in sweat and clothes strewn everywhere, minutes after they entered the room. Moans and groans could be heard in the hallway as other lovebird guests made their way to their rooms. Janice could not be silenced as Chauncy made love to her all over every piece of furniture in the room. From the edge of the bed, to the loveseat in the living area, the desk top, and the hot tub, Janice was pleased over and over and came more than she ever thought she could before falling asleep in Chauncy's arms until later that evening. They ordered room service, as the two of them were hungry. After eating a very late dinner, they acted like two teenagers fucking all night long like rabbits.

The first day at the resort was so good; the lovebirds were preparing themselves for an encore the following day. Exhausted from being oversexed the night before, Chauncy and Janice slept all night. It was around seven o'clock in the morning when Chauncy woke up and walked to the bathroom, leaving Janice, in what he thought, was deep sleep. Janice had never been a hard sleeper. The slightest movement on the bed would wake her up. The fact that she also needed to urinate forced her to leave her comfortable spot on the bed to head to the bathroom. All was quiet as she stepped toward the bathroom and swung open the door. Janice was shocked to find Chauncy on the bathroom toilet with an intravenous needle in his arm injecting a dark substance into his vein while his eyes remained closed. He never even heard the footsteps as Janice approached the bathroom. His only concern was the hit that he desperately needed. He was about to sigh when Janice asked, "What the fuck are you doing?" in an angry tone. Shocked and embarrassed, Chauncy tried his best to do some damage control, but Janice was livid. The first thing that ran through her mind was the fact that she and Chauncy had unprotected sex on more than one occasion. Her ignorance was at the forefront of her mind as she believed that he could possibly be HIV positive because of the use of needles.

Up to this point, Janice had not seen Chauncy's forearms in the light. His arms always remained covered when he was around her. He would only take off his shirt in the dark while they had sex and afterwards he would quickly throw on his long sleeve shirt and long pajama pants to hide the needle tracks on his arms and legs from her. Janice couldn't believe what she was seeing; the malignant veins on both arms and the open wounds were enough to scare a drug therapist. "Take me the fuck home!" Janice screamed while walking back to the room to gather her belongings. Chauncy chased after and said, "I can explain. Baby, please don't be mad." "Is this what the fuck you do in your free time? This some kind of shit musicians do? What, are you fucking Ray Charles? I ain't gonna be the one," the diatribe went on as she packed her stuff. Chauncy didn't know what to do or say because Janice was so angry. He retreated and allowed her the time to compose herself and gather her thoughts. After packing everything, she jumped in the shower. While in the shower, Janice shed more tears than water beads hitting her body. Just when she thought she had found the perfect guy, he turned out to be a junkie. She was angry and couldn't understand why her world was collapsing at once. She came out of the shower to find a sobbing Chauncy on the floor by the bed like a child, with his head between his legs, sulking a little. He knew he had just lost the best woman he could've ever found. Janice felt pity for him. The room was silent as Janice got dressed, so Chauncy could take her back to New York. He said nothing to her. "Aren't you at least gonna tell me why you're doing this to yourself?" she asked with tears streaming down her face. Janice had no idea the struggle that a heroin junkie faced daily, because she had never been around one on a personal level. True, she had seen the crackheads not too far down the street in the projects near her neighborhood, but she never interacted with them. By the time Jackie's crack addiction was full-blown, she had decided to move out of the house to keep it from her mother. She hung out in crack houses and never allowed her mom to see her when she was high. Janice never even knew that her daughter was a crackhead until it was too late. Chauncy couldn't even look at Janice straight in the face to offer an explanation. However, he felt that he at least needed to tell her the history of his drug use. With his head bowed towards the floor, Chauncy began to explain his addiction to Janice and his fight to rid himself of his daily habit. By the end of his conversation, Janice had a clearer picture and empathized with Chauncy a little more than before. However, she wasn't gonna sit around and watched him destroy his life. She promised she would help him get clean.

Welcome To The World Of Demons

The process of getting clean from drugs is usually easier said than done. Janice had promised to help Chauncy get clean, but it was up to Chauncy to enroll himself into a rehab center to receive the adequate services he so badly needed. After searching the New York area for care, Chauncy found an outpatient rehab center in Manhattan that was "convenient" for him at Hazelden on 8th Avenue in Chelsea, near his home. Though the program recommended their intensive inpatient care to help wean him off heroin, Chauncy used the excuse that he had to earn a living at the club to participate in the outpatient plan instead. In the meantime, Janice's problems were mounting as she discovered that her daughter had become a full-blown crackhead. Janice barely recognized Jackie when she came home one day after being out of the house for almost six months, doing God knows what. Her hygiene was nonexistent. She reeked of a foul odor that Janice couldn't fathom. The first thing she did was offer a bath to her daughter. Janice was sad to see her only daughter looking like she had been homeless. Her brown-stained teeth, discoloration of her once-beautiful complexion, dirty hair, and filthy clothes forced a kneejerk reaction of tears down Janice's face. She couldn't believe her baby was so far gone.

As the bills continued to pile up, Janice didn't have much of a solution to her problems. Kwame was in love and thought that everything was fine at home. He continued to send money home, but it subsided a little after he met Sandrine. Because he always paid half of Sandrine's airline ticket when she visited him, he had less money to send home. He also wanted to build a nest egg so he and Sandrine could start a life together after he got out of the Navy. Janice didn't want to burden her son with her problems. She was happy that he had found somebody special that he told her she was going to meet very soon. Kwame was excited when he called his mom to tell her about the African goddess he met in Paris. He described her to his mom and even compared her positive attributes to his mother's. Janice shared in his excitement and she never revealed her own struggle back home.

Now that Jackie was back, Janice wanted to help nurture her daughter back to a presentable state. After Jackie took her bath, Janice washed her hair and cooked her some food. Jackie ate like she hadn't seen food in years. She was a lot cleaner than she was when she first came to the house. She still had clothes left in the closet in her room, so she changed into some clean clothes and shoes before sitting down in the chair in the kitchen for her mother to do her hair. Her wet curly locks were braided into cornrows. Janice was happy to see her daughter cleaned up, but she didn't know that Jackie would be wearing these clothes without taking another shower until she saw her again. Like most addicts, Jackie didn't just come to see her mother, she also came to get money to feed her addiction. Janice had watched enough movies to know that she couldn't allow Jackie access to the very little money she had left in the house, so she took her last $300.00 and placed it in her bra, a place Jackie would have to invade. Things were a lot more difficult for Janice in the summer, because she couldn't sub. She was able to get odd job placements from a temp agency she signed up with at the end of the school year. Jackie begged her mother for $20.00 before making her way out the house, but not before grabbing a DVD player, hiding it in a bag of clothes that she pulled from her closet. "Ma, I will see you later," she said as she made her way out the house. "When am I gonna see you again?" Janice sadly asked. "I don't know, but I love you," Jackie said hurriedly before dashing for the door. Jackie couldn't wait to get to the crackhouse to sell all the items she had taken from her closet for drugs. She knew she had enough money to get high for the rest of the night. Getting money to buy drugs had become harder for Jackie and her friends. As her beauty faded and her life drowned in the belly of the beast, her sexual favors were not in high demand anymore.

Little Rob had taken beautiful Jackie and turned her to a crackhead who would suck all of his boys' dicks for a rock and peed on her to humiliate her because she didn't go out with him in high school. It went from having threesomes with her friends and graduated to utter degradation as Jackie's addiction to crack got out of control. Little Rob relished in the moment the first time he got a blowjob from Jackie for a rock. He took her to the back room and forced her on her knees while he captured it on video camera. Jackie sucked his dick until her jaw hurt. Little Rob could be heard on camera calling Jackie all kinds of degrading names as she took his dirty dick in her mouth. "Suck it, you crackhead, hoe. I bet your college boy never had you suck his dick like that," he humiliated her. When he was about to cum, he acted like a porno star and pulled his dick out of her mouth and spread his semen all over her hair. He threw the crack rock on the floor where she searched aimlessly for it like a hungry dog. There were times when Little Rob forced Jackie and her crackhead friends to eat each other on camera for crack. He didn't keep those tapes private either. He would have viewing sessions with his friends at his house and laugh at the expense of Jackie. When Jackie could no longer perform sexual favors for Little Rob because she had become a thing of the past, she turned to prostitution on the street. When the prostitution market dried up because of her deteriorating beauty, she started sucking the dicks of her fellow crackheads for a hit off their pipes. If Janice only knew what her daughter had been through the last few months.

Janice was sad and disappointed after her daughter left. She had promised Chauncy she would come and spend some time with him. She took a shower, got dressed and went to Manhattan to be with her man. Unlike Jackie, Chauncy was fully functional and looked nothing like a junkie. However, when she showed up to see him that day, he had just injected himself with a hit of heroin. For some reason, Chauncy was more charismatic and uninhibited under the influence of drugs. After sitting on the couch with Chauncy telling him all that she had been going through the last few months, he also took his turn explaining to Janice why he started using drugs and the illusion the high provided for him, she became curious. She empathized with him. He made it sound as if his problems didn't exist when he was high. He painted such an insouciant and relaxing picture for her, she was willing to try it to get rid of her own problems. "Now, I'm not telling you that you should try it, but it can help change your mood and give you peace of mind," he said with reservation in his voice.

Janice thought about the consequences of getting high and quickly dismissed it as evil and devilish. She had just seen the state that her daughter was in and no way would she allow herself to get like that, she thought. "I'm not trying to be strung out like my daughter. She looked a hot mess when I saw her. That crack can ruin somebody," she told Chauncy. "Uh baby, no, no. This ain't crack. Crack is for broke people. This right here is grade A stuff. Pure," Chauncy tried to set some kind of hierarchy for drug use and Janice bought into it. "When was the last time you were tested for AIDS?" she asked with apprehension. "Why did you ask me that? I told you before, I don't share needles with anybody," he told her while motioning her towards a drawer filled with unused needles. "So you're just gonna stop your rehab? I can't be part of that," she told him. "You know what? I think you need to relax. Let me get you a drink," he offered. She accepted his shot of whiskey and her guard started to come down. One thing led to another after two more drinks and Janice was now sitting in Chauncy's living room with his belt wrapped tight around her arm, a needle in it, her eyes closed and feeling like she had never felt before. That was the beginning of the end for Janice. She and Chauncy went on a heroin binge all weekend, partied and sexed each other all day long.

Over time, Janice became addicted to the drug just as much as Chauncy. Though Chauncy helped pay some of her bills, Janice rarely spent any time at her place. She had become Chauncy's "get high" partner. The two of them were inseparable. It didn't take long for Chauncy to start depleting his savings, supporting the drug habit of two people. He was used to the high life and now he had a partner in crime that he also had to support. After a while, Chauncy started missing his gigs at the club. The rest of the band members were always mad at him, but they could do nothing about it because it was his band. However, once he started choosing getting high over his gig at the Blue Note, his contract was terminated. Word started to spread about his addiction and no other club in New York wanted to take a chance on him. Chauncy's life was now on a downward spiral and getting out of control fast. Janice's life was no better.

A Sad Reality

While Janice continued to neglect herself and her home, Jackie was cleaning it out. Jackie went by the house every week to find household goods, furniture, appliances and electronics to sell to the dealers, so she could pay for her drugs. Janice didn't care too much at that point because her own life was out of control. The more time she spent with Chauncy, the more time she wasted getting high. Janice and Chauncy hit rock bottom after Chauncy lost his gig and completely depleted his savings. A few of his old associates would look out for him occasionally, but behind his back they labeled him a junkie. As word spread about his out-of-control addiction, some people stopped answering his calls and even more changed their numbers. Chauncy was isolating himself from the world and all the people who cared about him. Even his mother was frantic when she didn't hear from her son for a while. Things would get worse after Chauncy stopped paying his mortgage. The bills started to pile up all over the house. He and Janice were now living in total darkness as his electric was cut off. His only concern was finding money to get high. As Chauncy's financial bolts started to tighten, desperation started to set in. Most of his designer clothes, shoes, electronics and appliances were sold and his place was completely empty, the only thing left was his mattress. He even sold his bed frame and anything of value in his loft. The wonderful relationship with Janice was also starting to get rocky. Chauncy wanted Janice to start contributing money to get heroin. For the first time in their relationship, Chauncy decided to go home with Janice to see if she had any valuables at her home she could sell. Since neither of them had any money, they both had to jump the turnstile in order to catch the train to Brooklyn from Manhattan. It was a funny scene because Chauncy and Janice had never been juvenile delinquents and never did anything illegal prior to their drug addiction. Janice didn't even know how to be a look-out while Chauncy tried to sneak through. They got caught twice by agents and had to walk down to another train station and mustered the courage to just jump and kept running. They got lucky. When Janice got home that evening, she was pissed. Jackie had already cleaned house and sold everything in the home of value. It was a wasted trip and Chauncy was heated. The house was deplorable. Since they had no money to get back to Manhattan, Janice suggested that they spent the night at her house. "I'm not staying in this dump!" Chauncy proclaimed. "Don't be calling my house a dump!" Janice replied. "Well if the shoe fits," Chauncy said sarcastically. "If we don't stay here, how we gonna get back to Manhattan? We ain't got no money," Janice reminded Chauncy. A quarrel ensued between the two junkie lovebirds, but they eventually decided to jump over the turnstile at the train station in Brooklyn to get back to Manhattan.

Once in Manhattan, Chauncy was able to call for one last favor from a friend that he had no idea was envious of his past life. This man had held a grudge and animosity towards Chauncy since his days in the R&B music world. Nevertheless, he remained a "frenemy" (a friend who's truly an enemy) to him. Since desperate situations call for desperate measures, against his better judgment or any judgment at all, Chauncy made that desperate call to his friend to see if he could score him some smack. The "friend" was more than happy to deliver. He and Chauncy made plans to meet in an isolated spot on 25th Street not too far from the Lower Chelsea Housing Projects. The man was elated to see that Chauncy had turned to a junkie. "So, what you willing to do for this smack?" he asked Chauncy sarcastically. "Man, you know I'm good for it," Chauncy told him. "Oh no, my brother, what you good for is to suck my dick before I give you my shit!" he said with a bit of disdain in his voice. Chauncy got defensive and angry, "Fuck you! I ain't no motherfucking faggot!" he screamed at the man. "Well, my man, if you want my smack, you better get on your knees and get to sucking some dick," he said with a grin. "I never knew you swung that way," Chauncy told him, trying to force embarrassment upon him. "I don't, but you sucking my dick will make it worth my while.

Do you want the smack or not? 'cause you're wasting my time," he told him. "I ain't sucking nobody's dick," Chauncy told him as tears welled up in his eyes. "Ok then," the man told him as he stepped out of the alley to make his way towards the street. Chauncy wanted to walk away, but his demons kept calling him back. The man had gotten less than a block away when Chauncy called out, "Ok, I'll do it. I'll do it, but I ain't no faggot." Chauncy was trying to reassure himself he was a straight man, but the needle had become a dick that he was willing to put in his mouth to satisfy his craving. The man stepped back into the obstructed alley, pulled out his dick and placed his hand on his waist while Chauncy sucked his dick until he came. He didn't even tell Chauncy he was coming because he wanted to humiliate him further. By the time Chauncy felt the warm liquid running down his throat, it was too late as he gagged and vomited all over himself. The shame that he felt at that moment was enough to drive him to suicide. He sat idle in the corner with his knees raised in front of him and his face buried in his hands. The man zipped up his pants and threw the small plastic bag with the drug on the ground near Chauncy. He was emasculated and humiliated in the worst way. It took all of his courage and strength to get up from the ground to walk back home to meet Janice, so they could shoot up.

When The Lord Calls

After Chauncy got home, he wrestled with the fact that he had to perform a shameful act in order to get high. Janice was happy when Chauncy threw the small ziploc bag on the floor towards her, confirming they had what they needed to get high. However, Chauncy was disgusted with himself. He walked to the bathroom and stared at himself in the mirror for a long time, thinking about how low he had allowed himself to stoop and how his life was no longer his true existence as a man. Chauncy also thought about the fact that his mother and the rest of his family looked up to him since he became the most successful person that they had ever been around. He thought about all those people who relied on him to be the perfect role model and example that his family members used every day, to set the standard for their own children. He thought about so much that he ended up punching the glass and cutting his hand in the process. Chauncy felt he was no longer a man.

In the meantime, Janice got everything ready, so Chauncy could start shooting up the drugs when he got out of the bathroom. The heroin was already in the syringe and ready to be squeezed into Chauncy's arms. Janice didn't have the patience to wait for him. She took her hit and left the rest of the drug on the floor while she enjoyed her high. Chauncy had brung enough drugs for them to get high for a couple of days. While Janice was dazed in the corner of the living room, Chauncy got ready to get high for the last time in his life. He knew just what to do to end it all and take himself out of the misery that had been taking place in his life. Chauncy was always aware of the amount of heroin he needed in order to get his fix. He had never mistaken his dosage in the past, but this time the extra large syringe would be filled to capacity and Chauncy injected it all in his vein, which caused him to drop to the floor and start foaming at the mouth immediately. Janice never had any idea that Chauncy purposely overdosed because she was too high to recognize anything. It would be the last time she saw Chauncy alive. The unforgivable homosexual act that Chauncy performed to get his drugs was too much to bear. He could no longer live with himself and didn't feel his life was worth living. Without leaving behind any clue for his action, Chauncy decided to go home to his maker. By the time Janice came down from her own high, it was too late for Chauncy. He was pronounced dead at the scene after the medics responded to Janice's 911 call.

Chauncy's body was shipped back to Chicago for his burial. His mother was sad that she had lost her son, but Janice was devastated she couldn't even attend his funeral. Janice had no choice but to go back to her home in Brooklyn after Chauncy died. She no longer had her friend, lover and heroin buddy. The loneliness was starting to take its toll on her. To make matters worse, Janice had no idea where her daughter was. Her house was in complete disarray. Everything of value in her home had been sold by her daughter to support her crack habit. The last pieces of furniture left in the house were sold by Janice, so she could purchase heroin. A family in need bought her old couch, and bedroom set. The only room in the house respected by Jackie and Janice was Kwame's room. For reasons unknown, they never tampered with the lock to pry his door open to sell his personal possessions.

　　After running through the money she had gotten from the sale of the furniture, Janice was once again dry and she needed to get high. She had no choice but to sell her worldly possession, which was her body. Janice never stood on the street corner to work as a prostitute out of respect for herself and her son. However, she performed enough sexual favors for the local dealers to earn the reputation and nickname "headbanger." The term headbanger was coined when Janice was performing oral sex on a dealer and she made him cum so quickly that he told her, "Your head game is banging. I'mma call you the headbanger." As word spread about Janice's special skills and her addiction to heroin, every small dealer in town was trying to score heroin just to feed Janice's need in return for a blowjob. However, one day while Janice's mind was clear, she realized what she was doing to herself and the humiliation she had caused her son, whom she still loved very much and respected. Just like Chauncy, Janice decided to take her life by injecting herself with more heroin than she needed for her hit.

Kwame In Europe

Meanwhile, Kwame was trying to maximize his benefits as an enlisting officer in the Navy. One of the benefits of joining the US Navy is the affordability to travel abroad. Kwame took great advantage of the perks and set out to see the world beyond what he knew in Brooklyn. Though Kwame wanted to, he couldn't trek across Europe like most white American kids with a backpack on his back. The melanin in his skin would not allow for such a welcoming invitation into the White Europeans' homes. He opted for a rental car instead. Kwame's arrival point in Europe was the Charles DeGaulle airport in Paris, France. It was his first visit to Europe. The formalities at customs were routine. Kwame's American passport and military ID allowed him through with no problem. He also travelled light, so his two carry-on bags were right along with him throughout the flight. No visa is required for Americans travelling to France. He decided to stay at a hotel located a couple of miles away from the airport called Hotel Campanille Roissy. Kwame expected a decent hotel for about 96 Euros a night, which converted to about $140.00 US dollars at the time. For that price, the average person in the US could stay at a 4 star hotel. After picking up his rental car from Enterprise, he drove straight to the hotel to check in. The time difference between California and Paris took a toll on Kwame's body and exhaustion started to set in. Having had to drive two hours from Camp Pendleton in San Diego to LAX and then take a ten-and-half-hour flight to Paris left him drained. Kwame left Los Angeles at 11:00 PM and didn't arrive in Paris until 6:30PM. The nine hour difference in time caused total confusion for him. He stayed up throughout the flight reading Sun Tzu's book called, *The Art of War*. Kwame immersed himself in the book so much he didn't realize the flight had taken so long. Completely exhausted from lack of sleep, Kwame couldn't wait to lie down on a king-size bed to get some much needed rest. After walking into the room, Kwame was shocked to find that European hotel rooms were designed as a necessity, and not a luxury. Everything in the room was pretty basic: a small room equipped with a double bed, a television, a small dresser and a bathroom fit for only one person. The European electrical outlets weren't even suited for his electronics that he brought from home. He couldn't even charge his cell phone. He had to request a special device to plug into the wall in order to charge his phone. Too tired to complain about anything, Kwame got on the bed and fell asleep within minutes.

Kwame ended up sleeping until the next day. Just like a military man, he got up in the wee hours of the morning for a four-mile jog. He got to experience the calm of Paris early in the morning. Traffic was limited as he jogged along a main highway while listening to his favorite tunes on an MP3 player with his headphones in his ear. A few white Parisians were surprised to see a black man running so early in the morning in an isolated area. Kwame paid no attention to any of them. Jogging was part of his morning routine and he wouldn't feel right throughout the day if he didn't do it.

Kwame was well-rested and ready to see what Paris had to offer. He got dressed in his basic blacks, black jeans, black sneakers and black shirt, and grabbed his camera before heading out to venture into the city. One of the most popular places in Paris is Champ Elysee, and Kwame wasted no time figuring out how to get there on his map. Kwame was still old school with the map. GPS was for sissies, according to him. After figuring out the route, he pulled out the parking lot in the rented Peugeot to get to his destination. He found it odd that the streets in Paris are so small, but so are the cars. He wondered how a family of five could travel anywhere in these little bitty cars. Kwame was amazed when he finally made it to Champ Elysee. The square was packed with international tourists. He was able to find parking after circling around for almost twenty minutes. He stepped out of his car with his camera around his neck just like a tourist. The boutiques lined up the street and the rich folks came to spend their money. Louis Vuitton, Gucci, Armani Exchange,

Chanel and every other top designer has a shop on Champ Elysee. Skinny, tall white women were everywhere shopping and spending ridiculous amounts of money on handbags. At first, Kwame intended to get Louis Vuitton bags for his mother and sister, but after a quick browse, he realized he would be bankrupt. He went to check out the Arc De Triomphe. Those damn bags were just too expensive. The Eiffel Tower snow glow will have to do.

After leaving Champ Elysee, Kwame drove down to see the Notre Dame cathedral. Apparently, the Catholic Church plays a big role in Paris and these humongous cathedrals were sprawled everywhere. People lined up to get a glimpse of the world's oldest church and best architecture. These churches were over two hundred years old and the craftsmanship on the columns, walls, and ceilings was just phenomenal. To think that architects were this advanced over two hundred years ago was mind-boggling. He took pictures and enjoyed the scenery. After visiting four different churches within a two-mile radius, Kwame had seen enough. He was getting hungry, so he went to this brasserie for a bite to eat. While he was sitting there waiting for his food, this stunning model-looking woman with strong African features kept looking his way and smiling. The woman was so striking Kwame didn't believe she had any interest in him. Her closely cut hairstyle exposed her high cheekbones, succulent lips, beautiful African nose and gorgeous dark brown eyes. Her sparkling teeth were white as snow and Kwame was smitten. Since his arrival in Paris, Kwame didn't meet too many people that spoke English and his French was limited. Having taken French for three years in high school without much practice since, "Parlez Vous Anglais?" was about all he could say. He was trying to muster the courage to ask the beautiful young lady to join him for lunch, but he didn't want to get rejected. He thought that maybe it was part of French culture to be overly polite and flirtatious. After all, most French people think Americans are rude. However, Kwame should've realized that flirting was an international language and there are no barriers to understanding it. The African beauty continued to sip on her coffee while her eyes fixated on Kwame every time he looked up. It had been a couple of years since Kwame joined the Navy and his body had matured to the point where women started to take notice. The rigorous physical training provided by the Navy only added to the perfect body that Kwame had started to develop since high school. His shoulders became broader, he gained an additional fifteen pounds of muscle, abs became more defined and he looked more like a man. It would be nice to have a companion while he was in Paris, Kwame thought. His soldier instincts kicked in and he decided to become a soldier of love. He got up and walked over to invite the woman to join him at his table. "Excuze moi, would you mind joining me for lunch?" he said, suddenly developing a French accent in the process. Kwame had never sounded more stupid. She looked at him and smiled. Americans for some reason always try to talk with an accent when talking to foreigners, the woman noticed, but she took it in stride. "Are you French?" she asked jokingly in English with a French accent. "No. I'm American," he responded. "Then why are you trying to speak with a French accent?" she asked, sounding sexy as hell to him. "I'm sorry. I really don't know why, but I see that you're fluent in English," Kwame said all excitedly. Again, she smiled at his excitement. "I would love to join you for lunch," she finally told him before getting up to move to his table. Kwame was in awe as this beautiful amazon of a woman got up and started strutting towards the table in front of him. She towered over him at 6ft 3inches tall in heels. Her curves were so nice and tight; engineers would want to study her before designing aerodynamic cars. Kwame walked slowly behind as he admired her perfect round booty, very small waist, baby-making African hips and thighs, flat stomach and perky C cups. Her dark chocolate skin glistened under the light. Her body was a clone of Serena Williams.

"What is your name, and where are you from?" Kwame asked after pulling the chair out to allow her to sit. "My name is Sandrine, and I'm from Cote D'Ivoire" she told him. As an American, he automatically assumed she was from France because she lived in Paris. He didn't quite understand where she said she was from, but he foolishly asked, "What part of France is that?" She shook her head as if to say he was silly. "Cote D'Ivoire is not in France, it's in Africa. I'm sorry. I think it's called Ivory Coast in English," she corrected herself. "Uh, you're from the Ivory Coast, ok. I hope to make it there one day," he said assuredly. "Excuse me, how do you pronounce your name again?" he asked politely. "It's san-dreen," she said slowly. "Ok, I got it. Sandreen," he said confidently. She smiled at the way he pronounced her name with his Brooklyn flair added to it. "What does your name mean?" he asked. "Well, the name derives from the commonly known Greek name Alexandra and English name Sandra. It means man's defender. It's a popular name in my country" she said timidly. Kwame shook his head and said, "Man defender, huh? Are you always gonna defend me?" he was trying to crack a joke. "Only if you need my help, but you look like you're strong enough to handle yourself," she said cracking back. The more she spoke, the sexier her accent sounded to him. "I've told you quite a bit about me, but you have yet to tell me your name," she told him. He was taken aback by his rudeness. "I'm sorry. My name is Kwame and I'm from New York, Brooklyn, New York," he said in his thickest cocky Brooklyn accent. He was so confident when he said Brooklyn, she smiled at his arrogance. "New York…I wanna visit there one day," she said. The chitchat continued and Kwame explained what his name meant and its origin to her. He was elated to find someone in Paris that spoke English. Sandrine was very easy to talk to. Kwame and Sandrine had a light lunch comprised of ham and cheese croissants. After they were done eating, Kwame was afraid he wouldn't see Sandrine anymore. "Do you live near the area?" Kwame asked hesitantly. "I don't live in the center of Paris, but I'm not too far, only about forty minutes away. I live in Evry, Ile De France," she responded cordially. "Well, if you don't have anything planned for the rest of the day, would you mind joining me on the rest of my tour?" Kwame asked, hoping to get a positive answer. "How about you tell me what you're interested in seeing, and I'll be your tour guide?" she offered while exposing her pearly whites to him. It was just what Kwame was silently praying for. He pulled out his map and showed her all the places he planned on visiting before leaving Paris to drive to Milan, Italy.

Sandrine and Kwame ended up spending three weeks together, exploring Paris, Milan and London. Kwame got to know Sandrine much better throughout his first three days while she showed him the best of Paris. They visited the Louvre museum, the Eiffel Tower, Montmartre, an old district of Paris on a hill where the Basilica of the Sacre Couer and the Place du Terre are located, The Panthéon - church and tomb of a number of France's most famed men and women, Centre Georges-Pompidou - hosting the Paris Museum of Modern Art, Palace of Versailles- the famous former palace of French kings and many other national sites that Kwame wouldn't have found on his own. The fact that Sandrine spoke the native tongue of France also helped greatly. She was very resourceful and the best guide that Kwame could've found. It seemed as if the two of them couldn't get enough of each other. Coincidentally, Sandrine was on vacation during the three weeks that Kwame was visiting Europe. She was enrolled at the University of Paris-Sorbonne studying fashion merchandising. Since Kwame wasn't into clubs much, he and Sandrine decided they would check out some of the best affordable restaurants Paris offered. Besides eating French cuisine, they also decided to check out a cabaret at the Moulin Rouge. The experience was fun and exquisite. The European vacation was very memorable for Kwame except for the overt racism he experienced when he was in Italy. There was one more thing to add to the list of what took place in Paris, Kwame also fell in love.

Finding Love In Paris

After unanticipated brief stops in London, Belgium and Copenhagen, Kwame and Sandrine returned to Paris. Kwame's departure flight to the United States was scheduled in Paris and he wanted to make sure he made the flight. He returned a day before his flight and it was that last evening together that he realized he was falling for Sandrine. Though the two of them had been spending all of their time together and sharing sleeping quarters, nothing physical had ever taken place between them. The sexual tension between them was undoubtedly there, but they never acted on it. Casual flirting replaced hot passionate romance fantasies as Kwame had made a promise to Sandrine before they left that he would not disrespect her. She appreciated him for that.

At night when Sandrine thought that Kwame was in his delta sleep, also known as the fourth stage of sleep, she would watch him as he slept for a few minutes, and then wander off to the bathroom to pleasure herself at the thought of Kwame bending her over on the bed and taking her from behind. Her soft moans could sometimes be heard by Kwame because he was a much lighter sleeper than she thought, due to his military training. As much as he wanted to make her fantasy real, he allowed her the privacy, respect and self-pleasure in the bathroom. He would smile to himself knowing she wanted him as much as he wanted her. He would occasionally touch himself at the sound of her moaning, but never had the chance to beat one out before she got out of the bathroom. One time she came back to pleasantly find a completely erected Kwame on the bed faking sleep. His shorts were filled to capacity with meat. It was the kind of endowment a woman dreams of finding in her man's pants. If they were in Africa, she would've made his endowment part of the dowry for marriage. Kwame was the biggest butcher she had ever met and she couldn't wait for him to start serving her all of his fresh meat. It was a joyous site as she imagined how she would ride his tool and allow him to please her when the time came. Kwame was packing some meat, she thought to herself. Her only wish was that he knew how to use his package.

Sandrine would find out how tasty and magical Kwame's magic stick was on his very last night in Paris. The sexual tension between them was at an all-time high. Sandrine had no idea when she might see Kwame again, and vice versa. They both looked like delicious marinated poultry to each other, while they stared endlessly into nowhere with thoughts of ripping each other's clothes off. Would it be too soon to let this woman know he was feeling her? Kwame thought to himself. Would he scare her off and she would want to leave the room to go home? An even scarier thought appeared. He shouldn't act out his urges because he could potentially ruin something great, he wanted to believe. Meanwhile, Sandrine was lying next to him wishing he would at least give her a kiss on her lips, or anywhere for that matter. Kwame kept applying pressure to his crotch so his dick would not get hard while Sandrine purposely got up to go use the bathroom, exposing her round booty neatly wrapped in boy-shorts below her sexy fitted spaghetti strap top, in the process.

She really could've gone in there to rub one out quickly, because all he heard was the sound of water running. She also never flushed the toilet when she reappeared from the bathroom. This little game between them was taking its toll. Kwame finally decided he would cross that line when he didn't hear her flush the toilet. He took off his t-shirt exposing his ripped chest and six-packs abs, like he was dangling a carrot in front of a rabbit. She took one look at him as she stepped in the room and her nipples became erected at his site. She wanted him. He wanted her. The two of them stared at each other for a quick second before Kwame pulled her towards him and said, "I'm sorry. I can't help myself. I want you so bad right now," while planting a kiss on her lips. "I was wondering what was taking you so long," she said as their lips parted for a few seconds between heavy breathing and tongue twisting. "You're a great kisser," she told him. "And you're the best, babe," he complimented. Kwame couldn't wait to feel her tight looking ass. He reached his arm around her waist and slid his hand down her butt, palming as much ass as his hands could handle. Sandrine was a physical beast. Her arms, legs and ass were as tight as a bodybuilder's. Kwame couldn't believe the firmness of her body as he ran his hands up and down, all over her while they continued to kiss. She also reached for his firm butt and ran her hands over it. The tingling between her legs was intensified. Kwame would have to tame her beast. Having been a soldier for the last few years, Kwame waited for the command from his commanding officer before taking action. "I want you to take me. I want you so bad," she whispered in Kwame's ear. They moved towards the bed and he placed her down on the edge with her legs spread wide. Kwame needed no more direction; it was time to get in the driver's seat. With her legs spread wide open and her boyshorts snuggling her crotch, Kwame kneeled between her legs and took a whiff of her sweet smelling pussy before gently prying his hand between them to rub her clit. Sandrine anticipated the movement of Kwame's tongue up and down her clit as her pussy juice invaded her course. Her closely shaven pussy had a purplish hue. The obstruction of the boyshorts would make eating her too difficult, so Kwame eased them off down her legs before burying his tongue in her. The meeting of his tongue with her wetness forced a slippery path in his mouth as he tasted her palatable juices. "Oh mon Dieu!" she screamed in

French letting him know how effective his tongue was. When she cooed in French, it only excited him more. "Baby, you taste so good," he told her as he over-extended and harden his tongue to go deep inside her. His tongue strokes were just right. She reached down to caress his bald pate while he continued to please her. Sandrine's over-extended clit made it easy for Kwame to please her. He slowly wrapped his lips around her clit holding it in place while he slowly caressed it with his tongue inside his mouth. The slow movement of his tongue around her clit in his mouth forced her into convulsions. "Je viens, cheri! J'arrive, bebe!" she yelled again in French while trembling to his ecstasy.

Since Kwame was not selfish with her, it was hard for Sandrine to act like she was. She wanted to reciprocate. She wanted to please him. The two of them switched position; Kwame now sat on the edge of the bed while Sandrine kneeled between his legs. His bulky shorts were about to explode. Though Sandrine had felt his hardness against her body while they were kissing, she could only imagine how long and thick his snake was going to be. He leaned back on the bed, positioning his elbows to carry his weight while his torso was up high enough so he could watch the pleasantry that was about to take place. She eased her hands up around his buttocks slightly pulling on his shorts to get them off. Trying to make it easy on her, Kwame raised himself off the bed to allow Sandrine an easy pull on his shorts. The shock in her eyes couldn't escape Kwame as

Sandrine's fixation on his dick and her sudden immobility caused her to gasp. "Wow!" she said in exasperation at the eleven and half inches of hard meat. She didn't realize that Kwame's package was so huge. She had never ridden anything that big before and now she was scared for having unwrapped it. It was too late now, she had already awakened the sleeping giant and now she had to take care of it. Just the sight of Kwame's dick alone was painful to her, and the reality of it inside her was even worse. "Don't worry, baby, I won't hurt you," he offered in comfort apologetically. She wasn't certain about his statement, but she was praying for the best. Kwame could sense the fear in Sandrine after she came face to face with his dick. "You know that we don't have to do anything. I'm good," he told her to ease her mind. "No, I want to make love to you baby, but I'm scared because your thing is so big," she said in a frightful tone. "I promise to be easy," he said while looking into her eyes and running his fingers through her short hair. The circumference of her lips didn't allow for too much intake of Kwame's overly thick and long dick. She eased her mouth around the shaft, licking slowly as much as she could before taking about four good inches in her mouth. Her tongue was soothing and therapeutic as she gently massaged his dick with it. "Yeah baby. That feels good," he told her. Though Sandrine was skeptical about her oral skills because she didn't have much experience, Kwame made her feel good as he was responsive and kind to her for her deed. As Sandrine got into the groove of things, she damn near forgot how big Kwame's dick was. She was sucking it every which way and found it in the back of her throat, hoping she could deep-throat even more than the eight inches already inside her mouth. "Your dick tastes so good, baby," she told him, sounding like a French sex kitten. "You feel good, too, baby," Kwame murmured, while under the spell of Sandrine. Throughout his life, Kwame had never been a player, but he slept with a few women since he joined the military. He had never met anybody as special as Sandrine and never felt a special connection to any woman until Sandrine. As far as he was concerned, the sex was just the cherry on top. He wanted her to be his woman.

The oral labor of love had to stop because Sandrine's pussy was throbbing and she needed to get her fix. Her pussy had never been so wet and Kwame's intimidating dick still looked intrusive to her. However, it was an intrusion she welcomed because she wanted to get fucked, well! The best suitable position to ease her pain was doggy style and at the suggestion of Kwame, she raised her ass above the mattress and held on to the sheets for dear life as he started to insert an inch at a time inside her. It felt good for the most part, because her overly moistened pussy allowed Kwame easy penetration. At about a good eight inches of penetration, Kwame developed a rhythm to please Sandrine. Her smooth chocolate ass made it hard for him to resist pounding her, but he controlled himself. In and out, he slowly stroked her pussy. She was enjoying it and inched her ass back more after every five minutes to absorb a deeper penetration. The thick creamy excretion exiting her pussy was an evident sign that she hadn't had sex in a while. Kwame's condom was covered with the white layered substance. He stroked and stroked and she begged and begged. After twenty minutes into it, Sandrine had taken all of Kwame's eleven and a half inches and was well on her way to ecstasy. "That's it right there, baby. That's my spot," she told him as he rhythmically tamed her pussy. "Don't move! Stay right there," she begged when Kwame finally got to her G-spot. Sandrine worked her own winding rhythm until she almost dug her nails into the sheets, letting out a loud lioness roar as she came. Understanding that he may not get another opportunity to get his own nut, Kwame took advantage of the situation by holding on tight to Sandrine's waist and winding tightly against her ass to force his own bodily fluid to exit his body. The two of them collapsed in each other's arms and slept until the next morning, sweaty bodies and all.

Sandrine was sad the next day on the ride back to the airport with Kwame. She couldn't believe how happy he made her in such a short time, and how much fun they had. Kwame also knew he was gonna miss her, but from that point on, he decided he would spend all his vacation either in Paris or California with

Sandrine. He also became less concerned with his mother because her demand for money had increased. Though he cared about her, he wondered why she was leaning so much on him financially. When Janice started lying to him about why she needed the money, he suspected the boyfriend she mentioned to him was probably a bum who was trying to take advantage of her. Kwame only sent enough money home to cover the tax and insurance for the house every month. Kwame never went back home until he was honorably discharged from the Navy. He was a veteran and a Navy SEAL for life.

Welcome Back

The six years went by so fast Kwame didn't even realize his time in the Navy would be so abrupt. There was no re-gentrification taking place in Brownsville, Brooklyn when Kwame returned home from the Navy that summer. It was hard to drive one block without finding a couple of potholes that could potentially cause hundreds of dollars worth of damage to one's car suspension. Luckily, Kwame rode public transportation. The filthy streets of Brownsville had seen better days and less winos and drug addicts since Kwame left. Parts of Brownsville looked like a war-torn place deserted by its residents. Boarded up windows and doors were the results of subprime lending and America's top CEO's greed for more than their share in life. Very few homes were occupied on the street where Kwame grew up, and the vacant ones served as crack houses for the neighborhood's addicts.

Kwame was not ready for what he found when he came back from the military. The well-kept home he left behind was no longer in its pristine condition; his mother's hygiene was nonexistent and his sister was selling herself on the streets for drugs. He hadn't seen them, but in his heart of heart, he feared the worst scenario. Shock and awe was the reaction when Kwame first laid eyes on the beautiful home that his grandmother had willed to him. He wondered if he was on the wrong block when he noticed the light green house with aluminum siding he left behind was now an old, rotted, gray shingle covered depilated home. Kwame recognized the wooden front porch, but the storm door barely hanging on its hinges was not a familiar site. The skeletal stray dog lying on the porch barely lifted an eye when Kwame stepped onto the porch. The dog looked like she hadn't been fed in months, but her loyalty was forever present. Given the proper situation, Kwame would've probably wanted to pet the dog, but this dog looked sick, like she needed to be put to sleep. He hesitantly knocked once, then twice and three times. Nobody answered. Uncertain of what might have taken place in his absence, Kwame was a little apprehensive about setting foot inside the house. After joining the Navy, Kwame hadn't come home since basic training. He wanted to serve the full six years before finally making the decision to come back home to live with his mom and sister. And he had his reasons.

Since no one responded to his knock, Kwame decided to turn the knob on the door to see if he could enter the house. Fortunately, the door was not locked. Kwame walked in to find total filth from the front door and as far as his eyes could see throughout the house. He was still carrying his big military bag on his back when he started walking from the front door towards the living room, surveying the unanticipated mess. There was a musty odor throughout the house and Kwame could hardly breathe. He pulled out a handkerchief from his back pocket and placed it over his mouth as he walked through the house. As he looked around, he noticed that most of the furnishing was gone and only odd pieces of mismatched furniture were left throughout the house. There were no more matching chairs and table in the kitchen; the living room was completely empty. His grandmother's china was gone, every piece of furniture in the dining room was gone, and the beautiful antique lamps were also gone. It was almost as if a storm ran through the house. There were newspapers piled up on the floor, as if someone laid them out to make a bed. Kwame could only shake his head in disgust. Things would get worse as he made his way upstairs towards the bedroom. The walls were dirty and the entire second floor reeked of urine. It was no place for a human being to live. Kwame kept his military bag on his back the whole time. He wanted to get to his room so he could set it down before walking through the rest of the house. He kept calling out for his mom, but there was no response. Finally when he got to his room, he noticed that the lock was still intact. He had to use his key to get in. To his surprise, the room was kept the same way he left it. It was the only neat and clean place in the whole house. It was also the only time that he had realized he was really home. He still didn't believe that his mom had allowed the house to fall into such a destructive and repulsive mess.

After setting his baggage down in his room, Kwame immediately ran towards his mother's bedroom where the door was wide open. He was shocked to find his mother passed out on a dirty mattress with a needle still stuck in her arm. The once furnished room looked like a playground for the homeless. She appeared to be dead, as most of her vital organs weren't responsive to whatever test Kwame was trying to administer. "Mom! Wake up!" he screamed, but Janice seemed comatose. Kwame immediately pulled out his cellphone to call 911. He explained to the operator that he had just arrived home from the military to find his mom passed out. He didn't mention the needle he found in her arm. The 911 operator showed compassion for a veteran and immediately dispatched an ambulance to the house. It took about fifteen minutes for the ambulance to arrive at the home. It was then that Kwame showed them the needle that he found in her arm. The medics realized she was a victim of a drug overdose. Janice was given a sternum rub and she showed signs of life. The medics checked Janice's pulse, blood pressure and hooked her up to an oxygen tank. She was driven straight to the hospital. Kwame rode along with her, but not before he secured the lock on the door in his room and the front door of the house.

All Kwame kept thinking about on the ambulance ride to the hospital was how his mother was able to hide her addiction from him for so long. He talked to her regularly, when she had a phone, and everything seemed fine. The phone calls stopped after she told him she had to get the house phone cut off because she didn't want to pay an extra bill every month. She got a cellphone that worked for almost four years. It was towards the end of his tour of duty that Kwame had a hard time reaching his mother. She would always tell him that she lost her phone and he bought her story. The truth was she couldn't afford to keep a phone because her addiction had sucked her dry.

Kwame realized beating himself over the head wasn't going to solve anything. At this point, it was best that he prayed for his mother's recovery. Kwame never really got a chance to take a good look at his mother until the ride in the ambulance. There was a tremendous physical transformation that took place since he last saw her. Her skin was no longer radiant; her body weight had dropped at least twenty pounds, her beauty deteriorated; her hair was a total mess and her hygiene was altogether gone. There were needle tracks on every part of Janice's body where there was a trace of a vein. There was just a shell of Janice left. When he joined the armed forces, he left behind a beautiful and strong woman who had overcome so much. He started to blame himself for not coming home often enough to see his mother. Now, he also wondered where his sister was and how she was doing. He needed to find her.

Finding Jackie

Kwame was going berserk as he frantically searched for his sister. He carried a picture of her in his pocket as he walked around the neighborhood asking people if they had seen her. Kwame had no idea what he'd find when he did locate his sister. He wondered if she left the house because his mother had become a drug addict and she didn't want to be around her anymore. Every possibility was running in his mind, but his main goal was to locate her, so she could help him get to the bottom of it all. Kwame had no beginning point as he had no idea who his sister hung out with or what she was into. She certainly didn't have any friends when he was home, so there was absolutely no one he could reach out to. Kwame was hoping to catch a lucky break. After furiously searching for a couple of days, Kwame remembered that his sister had told him that she worked at the local supermarket as a cashier. He walked down to the supermarket to see if she was working there. Unfortunately, none of the workers there even knew who Jackie was. She had gotten fired so long ago, and the turnover rate for employees at the supermarket was so high, there had to be at least a hundred people hired after Jackie left. Fortunately, Kwame caught a break as he was about to walk out of the supermarket. The manager, who was also the son of the owner, spotted the curious Kwame through his one way mirror as he was enquiring about Jackie, showing his sister's picture to anybody who would listen. The pain and frustration on his face was the reason why the manager left his office and hurried downstairs to go assist him. "Excuse me, sir, I'm the manager here, is there something that I can help you with?" the manager asked politely. Kwame was relieved that someone finally offered to help. "Yes sir. I'm looking for my sister and I know that she used to work here a while back. Have you seen her around? Kwame asked with wonderment. He just happened to be at the right place at the right time. The manager paused for a minute and his face became flushed with sadness as he told Kwame, "Jackie used to be one of my best employees, but I don't know what happened." He continued as he stared at the picture, "I don't know if she got involved with the wrong crowd, but she was no longer the devoted employee and sweet young girl that I had hired. She started showing up to work late, high and sometimes completely disoriented. I had to let her go." "Do you know where I can find her?" Kwame asked with hope in his voice. "Well, I hate to be the one to break the bad news to you, but your sister no longer looks as sweet and innocent as that picture you're holding. The last time I saw her was a few weeks ago, and we had to have her arrested for stealing. She looked like a complete crackhead," the man told Kwame remorsefully. "My sister ain't no crackhead, bro," Kwame said trying to check the manager. "I'm sorry, man. I've been in this neighborhood for a long time and I can recognize a crackhead when I see one. You might wanna start looking around the crakhouses to find her. I'm sorry that I can't help you further," the manager said before walking back to his office to monitor his employees as well as potential shoplifters from his office.

Even though Kwame was disappointed with the news that he had received about his sister, he at least had a lead and knew which direction to go in order to find her. Kwame was angry and furious that both his mother and sister had become junkies. He had a dilemma in his hands. He didn't come home to face this kind of adversity. He came home hoping to become a firefighter like his dad had hoped, but now he had to alter his plans in order to keep his family from total demise.

The abandoned houses sprawled across the Sutter Avenue area, near the Brownsville projects, like weeds growing on an isolated farm. Kwame had no idea where to begin. The fact that his mother was in the hospital recovering from an overdose played a big part in his anxious search for his sister. He was elated that the doctors at the hospital told him that his mother would pull through, but he also worried that he might find his sister in the same state. Kwame wandered in and out of crackhouses throughout the area and never caught a glimpse of anybody that remotely resembled his sister. However, upon stepping out of the last crackhouse he had promised to visit for the day, this girl walked up to him and said, "I'll suck your dick for ten dollars, baby." Although Kwame didn't recognize the woman who made the offer to suck his dick, he knew that voice sounded a little too familiar to him. He turned his head around to find a crazy and dirty looking Jackie with dirty unkempt hair, smelly clothes, brown teeth, conjunctivitis in her eyes and a runny nose. She was completely unrecognizable, but she stood there and stared deeply into Kwame's soul before recognizing it was her brother. After acknowledging it was her brother, she took off running, feeling embarrassed. Kwame called out, "Jackie! Jackie, come here!" as he chased after her back into the crackhouse. Kwame couldn't believe what his sister had turned into. His once-beautiful sister looked like a monster.

Tears invaded Kwame's eyes as he walked down the street hauling his sister over his shoulder like a military bag. She kept kicking and fighting, but he wouldn't let her off. He wanted to take her straight to a rehab center to help her kick the addiction. Kwame had managed to save a lot of money while he was in the military. He was willing to take every penny he saved to help save his family. He took a cab straight from Sutter Avenue down to Seafield Center, a drug rehab center in Long Island, located in Mineola, NY. Kwame had been doing research to find a good rehab facility for his mother after she's discharged from the hospital. The Seafield Center's inpatient treatment was far enough from Brooklyn that his mother wouldn't have any distractions and he wouldn't have to worry about local negative influences on her. Now he also had to get his sister admitted to the center. Perhaps it was the best thing, because they could definitely use each other for support.

After some much needed convincing by Kwame, the center decided that they would make a bed available for Jackie. However, Jackie wasn't exactly the model patient. "Jackie, I love you and you're my only sister. This is for your own good," Kwame tried to convince Jackie. "I ain't trying to be locked up like I'm in prison, Kwame. I ain't your little sister no more. I'm a grown woman. I can make my own decision. You think you can just come home and start running shit again? Why the fuck did you leave us to begin with? I hate you!" she said while her eyes flooded with tears. The counselor pulled Kwame aside to explain to him that his sister's resistance to rehab and the animosity towards him was natural, and he shouldn't let it worry him. She fought the intake process and promised that she would run away from the center sooner or later. In spite of Jackie's belligerent behavior, the center still admitted her. Kwame's world had gone from happy to somber from the moment he set foot in his neighborhood. He couldn't believe what had happened to his family, his community and his neighborhood since his absence. He felt the need to do something about it.

Mama's Boy

Kwame didn't anticipate taking his mother and sister to rehab when he came home. He was only coming back for a pit stop before he headed out to Paris to stay with Sandrine for a few months after taking the exam for the fire department. Time with Sandrine would have to wait because his mama had to be first. Janice looked a mess in the hospital while lying in the bed with an IV in her arm. The paramedics got there just in time to save her, but more importantly, Kwame made it home just in the nick of time. She was happy to find her son by her bedside when she woke up from her state of euphoria. Kwame could sense the shame that his mother felt when she laid her eyes upon him. She felt that she had failed him as a mother and she didn't live up to the great example of a strong woman and role model he knew as a child. "Mama, there's no need to feel ashamed about anything. I'm here to take care of you and help you. I'm sorry that I never came home while I was in the service, but I promise I won't leave again," he said while staring in his mother's eyes. "I'm sorry, baby. I promise that I will do everything that I need to do to get clean. It's just that things have been so hard since you left..." Janice was trying to plead her case to Kwame, but he interjected and said, "Don't

- 165 -

worry about it, mom, everything will be fine. I'm gonna take care of you." Even though Janice was lying in a hospital bed, she was the proudest mom at the moment. Kwame saw the need to get up from his chair to give his mother the tightest hug that he could give her. "Mom, I want you to know that I have you set up for intake at an inpatient rehab center in Long Island the minute you are discharged from here. I don't want to take the chance of having you in Brooklyn," he told her firmly. "I'm going to do anything that you ask of me, son. You don't have to worry," she assured him. Kwame was glad that his mother was onboard with his plan. He told her he'd be right back. He went to talk to Janice's doctor and the doctor told him she'd be discharged the following day. Kwame immediately ran back to the room to tell his mother the good news. He spent a couple more hours talking to her before he left.

Kwame took notice of the fact that his mother looked like a bag lady when they brought her to the hospital. While he was visiting her, he made sure he wrote down her sizes in shoes, dresses, pants and tops. He also asked his mother what size his sister wore. After leaving the hospital, Kwame went straight to the mall to purchase clothing for his mother and sister. He had written down a list of items that they would need at the Seafield Center. Since the program is individualized for each client, he had to bring enough clothing that would last at least a week for his mother and sister; personal hygiene items such as deodorant, shampoo, toothpaste, toothbrush and other sanitary items for women; he had to leave $20.00 for each one for laundry, phone calls, detergent and vending machine needs; photo ID, insurance card, which they didn't have; and other miscellaneous things such as medication. Family participation was every Sunday from 10:00AM to 4:00 PM and Kwame promised to make it every Sunday for as long they were there.

Since Janice and Jackie had no kind of medical insurance, Kwame had to pay for the first week stay out of his own pocket, until the center verified that Janice and Jackie were qualified for Medicaid. He was relieved that they were qualified, because the travelling cost back and forth to the center was taking a toll on his savings. Kwame decided to buy a car to make the commute easier on himself. Kwame also had to deal with the repairs at the house while his family was in treatment. While he was in the military, he had become quite the handyman. Kwame wanted his mother and sister to come back to a livable home after treatment, so he spent his days and most of his nights repairing the house from inside out. It also kept him and his mind occupied while his family was trying to get clean.

The Frenemies

It didn't take long for Janice and Jackie's frenemies to show up at the house looking to score a blowjob for dope. These so called friends of Janice and Jackie's were their worst enemies. They were the force driving the habits of the two women. One day while Kwame was sanding the hardwood floor in the dining room, he heard a knock on the door. When he went to ask who it was, a man answered and said he was a friend of Janice. After opening the door, Kwame looked the man up and down as if he was taking close inventory of the man's mind. "Why you looking at me like that, bro? I'm just here trying to get a quick blowjob from headbanger right quick. I got my ten dollars," he said, showing the money to him. Kwame grabbed the man by the throat and threw him up against the wall. "I don't want you to ever step foot on my motherfucking porch again, you hear me!" Kwame told him before throwing him down the steps. "I ain't the one who got your old lady on drugs, bruh. You need to take your beef up with Little Rob. He's the one dealing it to her," the man said, as he quickly ran off before Kwame could whip his ass.

Kwame thought long and hard about what the man had said and realized if he could uproot the tree, the problem would be solved. More men would come to the house and Kwame questioned every one of them. The more he spoke with them, the more he realized they were just pieces to one big chess game. He also talked to his mother and sister during his visits at the rehab center. Jackie told her brother how she got hooked on crack and who was behind her addiction. Janice's story was a little different, but she also told Kwame that Little Rob had started supplying her with heroin as well, and he also had her doing demeaning deeds just to degrade her. Kwame knew just who his target was going to be as he set out to change the direction his neighborhood was headed.

A list of all the major players' names was drawn up and Kwame set out to take them down one by one. His relationship with Sandrine took a backseat because he needed to take care of home first. He tried as best as he could to explain to her that a family emergency had taken place in his family and he needed time to deal with it. He never once told her that his mother and sister were on drugs, because he didn't want to scare her. Sandrine came from a background of hard working people who didn't even know what crack was. He thought it was best not to divulge too much information to her.

By the time Kwame came back home, Little Rob and his crew were no longer small-time dealers. They had graduated and blown up to kingpins. Little Rob was at the top of the hierarchy. The BMW club was a thing of the past. The members no longer drove the same brand of cars, and BMW was at the bottom of their driving list. Bentley, Maseratti, Maybach, Phantom and Rolls Royce were the cars of their choice now. The crew was now "The Benjamins Click" and they were raking more money in the hood than Jewish and Korean business owners. Kwame watched the low-level dealers on the block everyday and took pictures of their transactions. He also took note of the rest of the crew that made their presence felt once a week in the hood. Kwame would eventually mark his enemies by a number on his list. They became known as the frenemies of the hood. Kwame called them frenemies because they wanted to appear as the Robin Hoods of the projects by having turkey giveaways for Thanksgiving and toy drives for Christmas, while selling their poison during the rest of the year.

Frenemy #1 was Little Rob. The name Little Rob of course derived from the fact that his father's name was Robert. Little Rob was not little at all. At 6ft 2inches tall and weighing about 190lbs, Little Rob was above average in height and stature. His name should really have been conehead because his head was as long as a cone, but he always wore a cap to keep it from people. Physically, Little Rob had very little appeal. Other than his crispy clean cut appearance and the brand name clothes he wore, there was nothing attractive about him. His nose was bigger than average, bulging eyes, thin lips and a long face that made him look like an ugly darker version of Gregory Hines. He was the leader of the click and drove the Black Rolls Royce, most of the time. His second car was a black Range Rover with tinted windows. Little Rob had worked his way to the top by using his street savvy, leadership skills and determination to prove to his teachers in high school, and all those who doubted him, that he had the pedigree to succeed. He was a hustler by nature. He was never a troublemaker at school or in the neighborhood, but he destroyed the neighborhood with his drugs. All Little Rob cared about was money because he grew up fatherless and his mother struggled to feed him and his two sisters. He wanted to change the situation for his family, so he turned to the dealers and pushers on his block for guidance. Those were his role models and his dream was to surpass them all.

Frenemy #2 was Smoov Kev. The smoothest and best looking guy in the crew, Smoov Kev was adored by all the ladies. He stood 5ft 10inches tall and weighed an even 180lbs. He looked like a pure athlete. Smoov Kev wore his wavy hair low with a well-maintained goatee around his perfect lips to highlight his light brown complexion, perfect nose and his light brown eyes. He was Little Rob's right hand man and he drove a silver Phantom. His second car was a Chevy Suburban. Smoov Kev earned his nickname because of his walk and his natural swagger from the time he was a young boy in the neighborhood. He would sway from side to side while he walked as if he was dancing to some kind of theme music. Even when he played basketball on the playground all his moves were fluid as he shot the ball. He was athletically gifted, but never cared about his academics. Smoov Kev initially was a distant admirer of Little Rob. He was impressed by the fact that Little Rob wore the freshest clothes to school, rocked the best sneakers, and owned a car while still a sophomore in high school. He made his admiration known and he quickly became Little Rob's "yes man." He would do anything to defend his boy as the friendship developed, and as a result, Little Rob allowed him to deal a little weed for himself on the block. Smoov Kev would do anything to prove his loyalty to Little Rob. He was probably the most dangerous member of the crew, because he always felt he had something to prove.

Frenemy #3 was Fat Black. At 6ft 8inches tall and 340 lbs, Fat Black was an imposing figure. The circumference of his gut created a protective barrier of fat between the world and his organs. A former offensive lineman in high school, Fat Black was deceptively nimble and quick on his feet, a deception he often used to his advantage. He did not look at all like a teddy bear. With a left eye hardly strong enough to function on its own and a big right eye with a slight red hue and flared nostrils, Fat Black could scare the shit out of a baby by just looking at him. His lazy left eye was the result of his rough play on the football field. He was the muscle of the crew and drove a white

Maybach. His second car was a GMC Yukon Denali. Fat Black earned his name because he was very dark and always fat from childhood. Kids used to make fun of him when he was younger, but as he got older and started standing up for himself, he always found a way to use his weight against his opponents. He overpowered most of his peers and that kept him victorious in many fights. Fat Black and Little Rob were childhood friends. They had known each other since grade school and the two were inseparable. He was always the biggest of the crew, so he instilled fear whenever the two of them got into a scuffle with anybody.

Frenemy #4 was Juju. The craziest of all the members of the Benjamins Click, Juju stood only 5ft 6inches and weighed about 150lbs. He didn't care about muscle or anything associated with physical training. All he cared about was his gun. He could take Goliath down as long as he had a gun. A straight thug who wore baggy jeans, fitted caps, sports jerseys and Tim boots, Juju was all about the streets. He had a medium dark complexion with an average build and average looks. An avid weed smoker and forty ounce guzzler, Juju was true to the game. He was the trigger-happy man of the crew. He drove a Bentley Continental. His second car was a yellow Hummer. Juju earned his nickname because he loved those artificially flavored .25 cents juices. He was always drinking them, so everybody started calling him Juju.

He was also a childhood friend of Little Rob and his loyalty was to the highest level. Juju became the trigger man of the crew because he was cold, heartless and calculated. He was all about living the high life, fucking as many women as possible, and anybody who got in the way of his crew was going to get it. Feared by all and respected by many, Juju shot and killed a man when he was just 14 years old. He was sent to a juvenile detention center and released at the age of twenty one. When he came home, he linked back up with Little Rob who promised to make him rich as long as he was willing to play his position.

Since Kwame had identified his opposition, it was time to start planning. Kwame didn't just want to take down the most ruthless drug gang in his neighborhood, he wanted to destroy them and make an example out of them. He wanted to eliminate the idea that becoming a drug dealer was a rite of passage in the hood. Also, Kwame believed that the United States government was the biggest culprit behind the push of drugs in our community. He wanted to fight the very system that trained him for the betterment of his community. Kwame was on a mission.

The Mission

Kwame hadn't been home long when he decided to take on the "Benjamins Click." They were his number one target, because word on the street was that the leader of the crew was the man who introduced his sister to crack. After taking out the first stash house, Kwame now had a bounty on his head. Though he remained a mystery on the streets and a legend to all who hoped for a better Brownsville, Kwame was already in too deep and becoming a hero was his destiny, whether he wanted to or not. One stash house was down and there were three more to go. Word about the incident spread like wildfire. All the drug users and dealers knew they were targets and feared the mysterious man of the night. There was going to be a lot of bloodshed on the streets, as many people were about to lose their livelihood as well as their lives in this battle over drugs. Crooked cops and dealers alike were going to be embroiled in this war against the scum of humanity. The drug dealers stashed guns everywhere in case of an ambush. Crooked cops walked around with "throw away" weapons in case their victims had to be set up to take the fall for them. There was hysteria on the streets and nobody in the drug trade was safe. A hero was born!

Kwame: An American Hero   Richard Jeanty

The man better known as a modern day "G.I. Joe" to many was all over the news. As stations scrambled to cover the story to increase ratings on the six o'clock news, the NYPD wanted to send a message of their own. They asked people to remain calm and no vigilante was going to be replacing them and take away from their good work on the streets. Channel 4 was the first station on the scene as flames cast a dark shadow of distress over the streets of Brownsville. Eyewitness accounts of the events painted pictures of a man out for vengeance, but he was kind enough to spare a few lives to send out his message so his story could be told. Kwame was clear that he wanted the streets of Brownsville to be safe and drug free for the benefit of the younger generation. He didn't want the next generation to endure the same thing that he did with his family. Naked women could be seen wrapped in towels as they scrambled from television cameras to avoid being identified as part of the drug gang in Brownsville. However, one woman agreed to relay Kwame's message to the media, as Kwame promised to come back and finish her off if she didn't follow through. A masked Kwame placed the .44 magnum on the back of her head while she laid naked on the ground, the woman thought it was the end of her days on earth. "Listen and listen clear, I want you to tell the news reporter that the streets of Brownsville are going to be cleaned and all the drug dealers will be wiped out. The cops can either be part of the solution or be a part of the problem," Kwame told her. She was scared enough to deliver his message.

Kwame wanted to increase scrutiny on the issue of drugs and instill fear in the hearts of everyone involved in drug distribution in Brownsville. With the aid of the media, he wanted to send out his message without ever having to come forward to reveal his identity to the police or the drug dealers. It was also his way of warning the police to increase their visibility in the community and to monitor the behavior of those men in blue sworn to protect and serve the people in the community. Kwame's mission was on the right course, but he didn't want any unnecessary casualties or anybody else to attempt to become a hero by duplicating the work he started. There would be no manifesto and no direct statement under aliases to any media outlet. His mission was to remain anonymous and his tactics innovative, because he didn't want the New York Police Department to associate his training with the military. There were few Navy SEALs in the hood and Kwame didn't want to raise suspicion on himself.

When Kwame joined the military, he told no one in the hood and he had no friends in the hood. He also asked his mother and sister not to say anything because he wanted people in his neighborhood to believe there was still a man in the house. Kwame never came home wearing his military uniform like most soldiers. In his neighborhood, he wore his civilian clothes because he didn't want to promote the military to young black men. He was completely against serving in the military because of the injustice he saw, the unfair treatment of minority personnel and the imbalance in ranks in the military. Kwame had decided against becoming a walking billboard for the military.

The Community and Family

Kwame had to wait until everything cooled down before embarking on another attack against the Benjamins Click. He had retrieved enough money from his last hit to help save a community center that was about to shut down, and another much needed community health center that serviced the poor and needy. The anonymous donations were greatly appreciated by both organizations. Kwame made sure to leave a note in the bag of money that he left by the directors' doors at the centers, warning them if the money didn't go towards the finances of the organizations, he would make sure they paid painfully with their lives in a diplomatic way. They were to call the media and announce the donations, so he could ensure the proper use of the money. He knew it wasn't the right way to offer financial assistance, but charity could sometimes lead to greed and Kwame didn't want to deal with greedy vultures who didn't put the community first. Checks and balances were also part of Kwame's plan as he tried to build a newly improved community.

Kwame realized there was enough money being generated in the community illegally that he didn't need to worry about finding a job. After all, it wasn't like the drug dealers could walk into a police station to report their missing cash. Each center received a quarter of a million dollars and Kwame still had another quarter million left from the hit. He contemplated buying a new home in a different neighborhood for his mom and sister to keep them from relapsing once they returned home from the hospital. However, he quickly scratched that plan because it would defeat the purpose of everything he was trying to do in his neighborhood. He wanted to rid his neighborhood of drugs and make it a safer place for families and children, and his family would have to set the example. Kwame also didn't want to draw any unwanted attention to his movement.

Kwame made the trip to Long Island every Sunday to go spend time with his family. An arrangement was made by the case managers to have Janice and Jackie share a room. While at the rehab center, the two women started to get reacquainted. Janice discovered a lot about her daughter that she didn't know. Jackie confessed to her mother how lonely she felt after her brother left and the nonchalant attitude that Janice displayed was enough to force her into the arms of evil. She told her mother that she often felt like the unexpected child that mommy had to accept, but didn't necessarily want. The fact that Janice always glorified Kwame as her hero to Jackie and other family members, made Jackie feel like unappreciated. Janice tried her best to clarify things for her daughter, but she also felt that her actions contributed to her daughter's detrimental behavior. During one particular visit with Jackie and Kwame, she tried to explain her position, "I understand how you could've thought that I love Kwame more than I love you. But you also have to realize that Kwame has always been the man of the house since your daddy died. He has always been my little protector and then he was gone. I missed him. I didn't realize I was taking advantage of your constant presence around me, and I'm sorry. I love both of you equally. You're my only daughter and he's my only son, I can't be bias towards either of you. I hope that you can forgive me." Janice got it off her chest as her emotions took over. Kwame pulled the two of them together for a hug. He dug into his goody bag to pull out two new outfits he bought for them. The case manager had informed Kwame of the fast progress his mother and sister had made and he wanted to reward them.

The six hours Kwame spent with his family every Sunday only reinforced his dedication to bringing them closer and making his neighborhood better, and to create a family-friendly environment for the people of Brownsville. Family time also became his refuge and solace from all that was going on in his head. Kwame had an uphill battle ahead, but he gave no indication of his thoughts and stress when he visited with his family. He was always all smiles and fun around his mother and sister. Detox was the hardest part of treatment and both ladies had gone through it successfully. Kwame was proud of them and he encouraged them to stay for an extended period of time to lessen the chances of a relapse. Kwame always left his mother and sister with a prayer, a hug and a kiss for each of them.

Ready For War

Another attack against the Benjamins Click was long overdue. Kwame had given them too much time to regroup and figure out ways to better protect their operations. A good percentage of Little Rob's business had been destroyed and he wanted to find out the crew behind the attack. None of the members of his crew wanted to believe the attack was by a lone person, as described by witnesses. "Man, ain't no way one man is gonna walk into my establishment and take out all my men, by himself. That's bullshit! Either we got a snitch among us that's leaking information, or he's working with an army of mu'fuckas," Little Rob told his crew as they met in his living room to work out a plan for a counter attack. The problem, however remained, he didn't know who his nemesis was. He was fringing on the dirty cops that worked for him who knew the outline of his building and the net profit of his daily operations. "It's gotta be that pig Spencer!" Juju spewed in anger. "He the only one who knows about that particular operation and he's the only one who's ever taken a tour of the place. That mu'fucka's not only strong arming us by taking a 20% cut every week, but now he wanna cheat us, too? It's time to murk that mu'fucka!" Juju was pissed and ready to put a bullet in

Spencer. "Man, we can't bring no extra heat on ourselves by murking Spencer. Whether or not he's dirty, he's still a cop and these motherfuckers get more adulation dead than when they're alive. We gonna have to be careful," Little Rob warned.

Little Rob met Officer Spencer when he was still a weed dealer. Spencer had stopped and frisked him a few times and even locked him up on misdemeanor charges for possession. Over time, the harassment turned to a partnership established by Little Rob after Spencer busted him with twenty pounds of marijuana. It was one of the biggest busts that Spencer had made since joining the force. Though the amount of marijuana could've earned Spencer a citation from the NYPD, the $20,000.00 in cash forced him to reevaluate his decision. The money was confiscated, he let Little Rob walk and a partnership ensued. Spencer was the lead officer of Narcotics in Brownsville and his arrest record was one of the best for the area. After entering into a deal with Little Rob, he opened the floodgates for more drugs to be brought into Brownsville. Officer Spencer's greed took precedence over his oath to protect and serve. He was netting almost $25,000 a week during the first year of operation when Little Rob switched from marijuana to cocaine. His arrest records continued at the same pace because all of Little Rob's competitors were being rounded up daily and brought up on trumped up charges by Spencer. On occasions when Spencer stopped a suspect who was clean, he would plant his own drugs on the suspect to keep pace with his arrest record. As Little Rob's business increased, so did the protection needed to move his product. Officer Spencer couldn't be everywhere. They needed more lookouts. Officer Spencer started recruiting some of his most loyal friends from the force who had a taste for the finer things in life.

By the second year of Little Rob's cocaine operation, Officer Spencer had recruited three additional officers to serve as informants, protection and lookouts for the Benjamins Click. Business was booming and the rival gangs didn't stand a chance of competing. There were four stash houses and the crew of officers netted $250,000.00 a month. However, Officer Spencer was paying close attention to Little Rob's operation. Every time the business expanded and profit increased, Spencer's demands increased as well. He was making $100,000.00 a month, while his officers took in close to $60,000.00 every month, only six months after recruiting them. Officer Spencer and his crew took trips out of town to Vegas, Foxwoods and the Caribbean so they could enjoy the good life and popped champagne like rap stars. Atlanta and Miami were their other two favorite destinations because of the endless amount of strippers and strip clubs in the two cities. Spencer warned his recruited officers not to be flashy in the city and to keep as low a profile they possibly could. He noted buying an expensive car was definitely out of the question. However, they were free to live it up outside of New York City. At times, Spencer even forgot that he was a cop. A 5ft-10inch and 185lbs rugged, medium dark skinned looking brother with a scar across his right cheek, black hair and a black goatee, Spencer definitely came from the streets. His vernacular was street certified and his swag had authority. Spencer was out to get his and he never hid that fact from anybody. Whether he was making thousands of arrests per month for the NYPD, or locking up rival gang members to increase his stake in Little Rob's business, Spencer was all business all the time.

Spencer's aggressive behavior started to create confusion amongst Little Rob's crew members after the stash house was robbed. They couldn't believe that Spencer and his boys would get so greedy as to betray them. "You remember how that mu'fucka rolled up on us when we were in your Rolls and he was all like, 'how much one of these cost? I think I need me one of them.' That was that envy right there. I knew that bastard couldn't be trusted," Fat Black told the crew in suspicion. Everyone shook their head in agreement. Spencer wasn't the only one who ever made that comment. A couple of the other officers had also made envious comments about increasing their stake in the business. Little Rob knew he couldn't just kill the officers without facing dire consequences, but he had to wait and monitor the situation. Killing a cop was a death sentence, something that Little Rob wasn't ready to face yet.

Meanwhile, Kwame had been staking out the streets and watching every move made by Little Rob and his crew from the attic in his house. He had set up special binoculars and cameras to record their every move. Kwame also took notice of the same four cops who kept locking up certain people, but turned a blind eye to a particular group. It didn't take a genius to figure out Spencer and his boys were dirty and working for the Benjamins Click. Kwame decided to focus on Little Rob's crew, as well as Spencer's crew of cops. The casual meetings between Little Rob and Spencer took place all around the city. The two would meet and discuss their plans for the week and Kwame would not be too far away, capturing everything on camera. Though he didn't have sound, the exchange of money between Spencer and Little Rob was obvious on camera. It was always the same bag of money on the same day that was handed to Spencer every week. Kwame knew something was brewing when Spencer and Little Rob got into an argument one day, and Spencer drew his gun on him. Obviously angry, Little Rob's lips could be read when Kwame zoomed in for a close-up, as Little Rob told Spencer to shoot him and get nothing from a non-existing business. There was a compromise of trust and a battle was brewing. Kwame was getting ready for war.

A New Strategy

Juju had been thinking what happened for a while. "Look, we lost a lot of our soldiers the last time we got hit by this crew, so this time I want us to be alert and ready when he shows up again. Since we've lost one of our spots, we're now down to three and I'm gonna need each one of you to stand posted at your spot. Juju, you're gonna be taking the fall for the last hit. You were responsible for that spot and your ass wasn't around to protect it. That's about a mil that you gotta pay back," Little Rob informed the crew. From the very beginning, Little Rob had delegated responsibility for each stash house to each member of the crew, including himself. Each member's weekly purse came from the money brought in by the particular stash house he was responsible for. Kwame managed to walk away with over a million dollars in cash from Juju's spot and an additional two million in product was burned to ashes. The crew already knew the rules and consequences had to be paid when the wrong decision was made. Juju wasn't too happy about his money getting cut and he didn't hide it. "What the fuck you talking about I gotta take that hit?" Juju asked in frustration. "Now, I told each one of you when we first started this shit that you were responsible for your own spot. It was y'all's ideas to have your own crack spot anyway, so I gave it to you, but the supply still came from me and I gots to pay the people who supply me with the shit. I don't expect anybody to cover my end, so I will expect that you would do the same. This shit ain't personal, it's business. You either have to finance a new spot with your own money, or you can take over my spot and double the profit that I'm making every week so you can get out of debt," Little Rob said firmly. Juju wasn't happy with what he was hearing, but Fat Black and Smoov Kev thought fair was fair. This conversation was the beginning of dissention among the group. Though Juju was careless, he expected the other members of the crew to carry his weight and have his back on his dumb decision to leave his spot. So much money was being made he never took the time to realize that he was part of an enterprise. Since the wheels were turning like clockwork, he figured he could just sit back and reap the profit of what Little Rob had set up for them. He always made his weekly quota, and numbers increased as his distribution surpassed expectations. However, Juju started slipping when trifling ass women became his priority. The Continental Bentley he was pushing gave him the notoriety of a rap superstar among the hoodrats of the projects. Juju was swimming in pussy everyday. He even took a couple of the hoodrats to his hideout in Long Island, something Little Rob warned him against. Juju didn't care. He had earned the reputation of a cold-blooded killer on the streets and he thought everybody feared him.

Juju was butt naked with sweat pouring down his body while still rocking his Tims as he fucked the hell out of this hoodrat named LaQuita. He was fucking her raw dog like it was the best pussy he had ever been in. Juju didn't fuck with bourgie chicks. If she wasn't a hoodrat, he wasn't interested. He and LaQuita had just smoked a huge blunt before she got on her knees, pulled out his dick and started sucking it. "Yeah, suck that dick, ma," he commanded. The slurping sound of LaQuita's mouth around his nine inch dick could be heard down the hall by her two children watching television in the next room. LaQuita didn't care. "Bend over on the bed. I wanna fuck you doggy style," Juju told her. "Come take your pussy, daddy," she whispered to him. Juju looked rough and rugged and he fucked her that way, too. He shoved his dick into her pussy and started pouncing it like she owed him money. "Take that shit! Tell me you love this muthafucking dick," he yelled at her. "I love it, daddy! I love your dick. Fuck me!" she screamed carelessly without any consideration for her children's virgin ears. Juju smacked her ass loud enough that anybody within earshot could hear the abuse her ass was undergoing. His long strokes came all the way down from his knees, like he was trying to wear out her uterus with his dick. LaQuita loved it, or at least she acted like she did. After ten minutes of hard stroking, Juju pulled his dick out for a backshot as he came all over LaQuita's ass. He didn't pull out often, but every now and then he felt the need to watch his semen splashed on the ass of a woman. With five children by five different women relying on him already, Juju didn't need to add another child to his family tree.

That was business as usual for LaQuita and Juju. LaQuita couldn't afford to stay in her section 8 apartment without the money Juju gave her every month. The fathers of her two children were both in jail for drug distribution and she was working on her third baby father who shared a similar background. LaQuita knew she wasn't the only chick that Juju was fucking on a regular without using protection, but it was a small price to pay considering Juju was her caretaker and provider. LaQuita was the typical light skinned weed-smoking hoodrat, rocking a long weave, a booming body, colored contacts in her eyes, with a closet full of bootleg Gucci, Prada, Louis Vuitton and other well-known designers. Juju kept her laced with the fake shit from Chinatown. For some reason, she believed he would spend a thousand dollars on a real purse for her while only giving her about $300.00 a week. He never let on that the items he bought her were counterfeit. Juju was doing the same thing for all his hoodrats. He bought all of them counterfeit clothes, purses, shoes and cheap hollow gold. He also paid to get their hair or weaves done weekly to keep them happy. That was all the hoodrats required, anyway.

On this particular night while Juju was fucking LaQuita, Kwame was fucking up his money. Most of his crew was killed and his stash house destroyed in his absence. By the time word got back to him about the hit, Kwame was long gone, along with Juju's money. Juju was pissed, but he didn't have a target to attack. The frustration between what happened and how it happened baffled everybody. The only viable suspects were the cops who knew everything about their operation. Juju's money was now short and somebody had to pay. His trigger finger was itching to shoot someone, anyone who was involved with the hit. "I hope we didn't lose that spot because you were knee deep in one of your project hoodrats' pussy," Little Rob warned him. "Man, I wasn't with no hoodrat. I had to go downtown to make a run," Juju lied. "Whoever it is that did that shit, I need to figure it out and we're gonna have to deal with them. I'm not saying Spencer wasn't involved, but we have to be sure before we get rid of him," Little Rob told the crew. All of them shook their heads in agreement. "For now, I want you all to beef up security at all the other three locations and keep an eye out for anything suspicious. I'm gonna try to figure out if Spencer was involved, and if he was, I'm gonna kill him myself. This shit is not just shorting Juju his money, it's shorting me too. I can't get a twenty-five percent cut of something that doesn't exist. Juju, I'm being kind because I'm only holding you responsible for a million dollars. If you got some paper stashed, you can use it use to pay me. Otherwise, I expect you to cover my spot and double my profits for the next month until you're ready to open a new house," Little Rob told him firmly. Juju couldn't understand why he was being held responsible, but he said, "I got you. It was my fault. I'll work that shit back up."

Even though Juju accepted Little Rob's term in front of the crew, he wasn't really comfortable accepting responsibility for the hit. A new plan was drawn for Juju to double the weekly take of Little Rob's spot. Little Rob never mentioned a word to his connect about what went down. Since Juju was his boy, he paid the debt out of his own money for Juju without letting him know. The supply for the burned-down house was now coming to Little Rob's house. Distribution needed to increase and territories expanded. Juju had to get back on his hustle. Pussy and the hoodrats would have to take a back seat.

Bloodbath

With the expansion of the business, came an exorbitant amount of deaths. Juju didn't follow protocol to inform Spencer about the new territories he planned on seizing from other drug gangs surrounding his. After all, Spencer was a suspect in his eyes. Juju was a man on a mission as he went around the hood on a killing spree that left ten people dead within a week. Spencer didn't know what the hell was going on as homicides in his territory doubled within a week. However, when he started noticing the workers working the new blocks, he knew that the Benjamins Click was behind the murders, something he just couldn't condone on his watch. Juju was maniacal as he worked to double the distribution within a couple of weeks, so he could be square with Little Rob. Everything he did that week, he did with anger. One particular kid was told to take his business elsewhere, but had the nerve to say, "Who the fuck you think you are? You can't fuck with the Money Click. We take mu'fuckas out." He had no idea who he was dealing with. Juju had two of his men drag the kid into his truck, they drove straight down to the Belt Parkway and got off on Erskin Street and drove underneath the bridge. When they got to the deserted field under the bridge, they pulled the kid out, and held him while Juju cut out his nut sack and his eyeballs. He then shot the kid in the back of his head and left his dead body in the bushes. The following day, Juju had a member of his crew hang the nut sack and the kid's eyeballs on a street sign where the kid used to stand to sell his drugs.

There is always casualty in war and Juju wasn't seeing the last of the kid's crew. They came back with a vengeance. After Juju took over the spot, he had two of his boys running that block for him. It took about a week, but the kid's crew came back, shot and killed one of Juju's boys and kidnapped the other. They took him to an abandoned field in Far Rockaway near the beach, where they cut off his feet, hands and ears before shooting him in the back of the head. His body parts were left hanging on that same street sign where Juju hung the other kid's nut sack. The battle was raging and the murders were getting more gruesome with each new case. A lot of heat was coming down on the block and it was messing with everybody's money. Now, Spencer was getting mad because his cut of the money was affected.

Little Rod had mentioned to Spencer about the new expansion into a new territory that Juju was responsible for. Spencer and one of his boys drove straight to Little Rob's old spot to find Juju. Juju met them at the door before they had a chance to enter the stash house. "I need you to come with me right now," Spencer told him angrily. Juju was resistant at first, but the dangling NYPD badges around Spencer and his partner's necks were enough of a warning for the two goons trying to come to Juju's aid to back off. "We can make this the easy way or the hard way. I can shut down your operation now with one phone call, or you're gonna take a ride with us," Spencer told him through clinched teeth. Juju sensed the seriousness in Spencer's voice and opted for the ride-along. Juju was patted down for weapons by Spencer and his partner, and found none before placing him in the back seat of his patrol car, which was strangely covered in plastic. After Juju got in the car, there was silence. The fact that the back seat was covered in plastic didn't even cross his mind. The two officers said nothing to him. In his mind, he wondered what they were planning or where they were taking him. "Are y'all gonna tell me what's going on?" Juju asked coyly. No one said anything, but the lock on the back doors of the cruiser clicked to the locked position. They reached an area in Queens where there was hardly any traffic; only one car had driven by since they got on this particular road. Officer Spencer began speaking, "We've had a good thing going for a while now, right?" Juju shook his head in agreement. Spencer continued, "We've been making a lot of money and I've been protecting you and the rest of the crew with no problems. Whoever you guys wanted removed from the streets, I got rid of them, right?" Juju again shook his head to agree with Spencer. Suddenly, Spencer turned his head around and said, "Why the fuck would you want to take matters in your own hand and start killing people on my streets!" Before Juju could even respond, the passenger officer pulled out a 9mm Glock and let out two bullets right in the middle of Juju's head. Juju never saw it coming, but his workers would have plenty to say to Little Rob about Spencer picking him up from the spot. After making sure no one was around, Spencer and his partner dumped Juju's body, wrapped in plastic, in the ditch, away from heavy traffic. They drove back to Brooklyn, joking with each other and laughing in the car about what they just did, like it was common practice.

The Chess Match Begins

The evening news anchor sat in front of the camera and reported, "A man identified as Jason Banks was found dead on a deserted street in Rosedale. It appeared as if the victim was shot point blank in the face, twice." At first, it didn't seem like news to the people who worked for Juju, because they didn't know his government name. Little Rob had to tell them that Jason Banks was actually Juju. Juju's body was found a couple of days later on the side of a back road in Rosedale. A couple of the goons from the stash house told Little Rob that the last time they saw Juju alive, he was leaving with Spencer. "That mu'fucka getting bold now. He must be tryna send us a message or something," Little Rob said angrily to the rest of his crew. "That pig killed Ju. We gonna have to get that mu'fucka, man," Fat Black said with sadness in his voice. Fat Black and Juju were forced to form a strong bond of friendship because Little Rob and Smoov Kev were so tight. Juju was Fat Black's little homie.

Little Rob was furious after learning of the death of Juju. He placed a call to Spencer to find out what the hell happened. "Yo, I need to holler at you. I'm sure you already know what's going on. We need to meet," he said to Spencer like he was some type of mafia boss.

"Who the fuck you think you're talking to, one of your little flunkies? You better watch your fucking tone when you talk to me. I know your boy got killed, but don't be trying to bass, muthafucka. I ain't the one," Spencer told him in as authoritative a voice as he could. "Man, I ain't tryna start shit. I'm just tryna get to the bottom of what's going on. You got some time to meet with me?" Little Rob asked cordially after getting checked by Spencer. "Give me about a half. I got some paperwork that I need to take care in the office. Let's meet at the spot," Spencer told him. Little Rob and Spencer always met by the abandoned Livonia station near the L train.

Little Rob didn't know what to expect as he prepared to meet with Spencer. He ruled Spencer out as the killer based on the conversation they had earlier, but he wasn't sure. Spencer pulled up at the spot alone to meet with Little Rob. The strap on his holster was unfastened in case Little Rob had any funny ideas. Little Rob jumped out of his Rolls Royce to walk towards Spencer. After the initial greeting and dapping each other like business acquaintances, Little Rob began speaking, "I'm not sure if you know anything about what happened to Juju, but my peoples is telling me that you the one that picked him up from the spot the other night before he turned up dead. I'm trying to get to the bottom of this. I know Juju can be a hot head, but he would never cross anybody." Spencer was attentive and quiet as Little Rob spoke. He was trying to figure out the intent behind the conversation. "Ok, I'mma tell you like this. I did pick up your man, just to holler at him. I wanted to find out why he's hanging mu'fuckas' nut sacks and eyeballs on my street corner. The discussion got a little heated and we agreed to disagree. He had me drop him off on one of the blocks that he just took over, because he didn't wanna hear what I had to say. I didn't want to do it, because I knew the consequences. He had beef with a lot of people over there, but your man thought he was invincible. You can't go around shooting people and not expect them to shoot back. After dropping him off, I told him to be careful and I went on my way," Spencer lied. Little Rob wasn't foolish enough to believe everything Spencer said, but the story was believable enough for now. "You know we're a man short now, so the money ain't gonna be like it was," Little Rob warned. Spencer had to gather himself before speaking. He took a deep breath and exhaled before moving closer to Little Rob's ears and whispered, "This ain't muthafucking 'Let's Make a Deal!' My money ain't got shit to do with how you run your business or who's not around to do the work anymore. My money is guaranteed for as long as your ass wanna remain on these streets. These are my streets and you got to pay to run them, understand?" The bass in Spencer's voice, even though he was whispering, was enough to shake Little Rob. "Yo, I got it. You'll get your money. No sweat," Little Rob assured him.

Meanwhile, it was dusk and Kwame was on the prowl. He knew he had the best chance to attack Little Rob's stash house while he was away meeting with Spencer. The tactics used this time would be different. There were too many hired guns for Kwame to just sneak up and start taking them out. He needed to create a diversion. This stash house was located next door to a vacant house that had just been foreclosed by the bank. The utilities weren't cut off yet. Kwame knew this because he had checked out the house to make sure it was empty and that the crackheads hadn't started moving in yet. Outfitted in his Army fatigue with a gas mask over his face, night vision goggles around his eyes, and a duffle bag containing all his necessities to complete the job, Kwame camouflaged himself with the trees, until he gained access to the house through the basement. Kwame knew if that house was left vacant for too long, the crackheads would make it their home soon enough. The only way to avoid having another crackhouse in the community was to destroy it. Kwame went inside, turned on all the gas pilots on the stove as well as the oven, and busted the gas line to the boiler allowing gas fumes to fill the house. He also brought an old space heater that almost caught fire in his house when he was a kid that his grandmother had asked him to put away in the basement. Everything was set for Kwame's next big hit.

Kwame was very calculating and he made sure his plans were foolproof. Before leaving his house,

Kwame plugged the old heater into the wall and counted the minutes before it started getting hot enough to catch fire. In order for his plan to go accordingly, he had to make sure every detail was covered. The timing was perfect as Kwame waited in the dark behind the tree for the house to explode within the allotted minutes he had figured out. The vacant house exploded on cue as Kwame threw a tear gas grenade inside the stash house through a window, forcing everyone to take cover. The impact of the explosion next door coupled with the tear gas, created hysteria. Nobody knew what hit 'em. Everybody in the stash house started panicking as they ran towards the door, rubbing their eyes, trying to make it to the nearest exits.   The mostly hired women crew ran out the house in their birthday suits. Little Rob made sure all the women packaging his drugs were naked at all times, so they couldn't steal from him. People were feeling themselves out to make sure limbs weren't missing as they ran out the house. All of the hired goons standing outside found themselves on their backs and helpless as the explosion took the wind out of them. The able bodies could only get up and run for their lives. Everyone was trying to get to the front door. Meanwhile, Kwame easily walked through the back door and hurriedly walked throughout the house gathering as much cash as he possibly could and stashing it in a duffle bag while breathing easily through his gas mask. He had also set a gallon of gasoline by the back door, to ensure the decimation of the stash house, once he was done. After collecting his money, Kwame walked through the first floor of the house, pouring gasoline on every wall and all over the floor before lighting a match and setting it on fire. He walked off into the night with his duffle bag over his back leaving no trace to be found.

The Heat Is On

The heat was coming down on the Benjamins Click. This second hit threw them for a loop. They were confused now more than ever. Little Rob couldn't blame Spencer this time, because the two of them were meeting when the hit took place. Somebody was out to destroy his operation, but he had no idea who his enemy was. Little Rob and his crew were paranoid. Though there was no casualty during this hit, the orchestration of the hit was above Little Rob's head. He knew he was dealing with a professional. The local news stations didn't make it any easier when they reported an angry vigilante was out to clean the streets of Brownsville, and his targets were the dealers and pushers of that neighborhood. People in the hood often talk about blowing up a house, but nobody had actually done it. The explosion shook the whole block and everyone was worried that it was a terrorist attack on New York. People took to the streets and started looting. Shattered windows could be seen in rows of homes on Sutter Avenue and every mother kept their children close to them to keep them from harm. The explosion had instilled enough fear in the community to the point where nobody felt safe in their homes. The S.W.A.T team and bomb squad from the NYPD were called to the scene to investigate the fire and explosion. It was determined by the NYPD that the explosion of the adjacent home could've been a diversion for the actual target, which was the stash house. It was also determined that arson was the cause of the fire in the stash house by the Fire Department. The NYPD worried they had a possible nut case they were dealing with and warned the residents to stay off the streets.

Every member of the Benjamins Click and every worker were looking over their shoulder, wondering when they were going to be taken out by this vigilante. Even Spencer started to worry about his own safety and the fact that the FBI was about to get involved in the two cases. Because of the nature of the attack, the Federal government decided to step in to assist the NYPD with the investigation. As the lead Narcotic Undercover Officer in Brownsville, Spencer had to brief the the FBI agents assigned to the case and offer every detail as to why a vigilante easily accessed a drug warehouse while the police sat by and didn't move to make a bust. Careers were on the line and prison was looming for the officers involved. As panic started to set in, Officer Martin warned Spencer he wanted out and he feared that the FBI was going to find out their involvement in assisting the Benjamins Click with their drug operation; all of them would end up rotting in a prison cell for the rest of their lives. Spencer didn't need the added stress. He had enough to worry about. Officer Martin made it seem like he was ready to start singing to the Feds and there was no way Spencer was going to let that happen.

Spencer told Martin he was overreacting and there was nothing to worry about. He told him he had everything under control and they needed to take a trip to Foxwoods to clear their heads. The other two officers, Nelson and Ramirez who were also part of the rogue officer crew, decided to come along for the trip. The reason for the trip was to get their stories straight and establish good enough alibis to weaken the government case against them, in case they were going to be charged. Martin felt more comfortable knowing all four officers were making a pact to stay the course together. The ride to Foxwoods was only a couple of hours from New York, but Spencer told Martin to tell his wife he was working overtime. Nelson had to tell his wife he was working overtime as well, since he was the only other member of the crew who was married. Martin's paranoia decreased a little, but his worried face could easily be cracked by the FBI.

Spencer knew the FBI was on them like white on rice and he had to find a way to shake them. He and Ramirez had made plans to meet on a street located two blocks from his house. All the officers involved were being tagged by FBI agents and they knew it. Ramirez and Spencer were partners when they first joined the Narc Unit and they remained close, since forming a bond at the academy. Looking through their records, the FBI knew if Spencer was going to recruit anybody he could trust to do something illegal, Ramirez would be his man. Martin and Nelson were also partners, but the two of them grew up in Hamilton Beach in the same neighborhood. There was nothing on their record to indicate they would get involved in anything illegal. Of course, that was before they were presented with the opportunity to make sixty grand a month, dirty money that was going to be paid by drug dealers they were going to protect.

As usual, whenever Spencer was home, the light in the kitchen would be on and the television could be heard in the living room. He left a mannequin lying on his couch holding a beer before sneaking out of the house. Officer Spencer left his cruiser in his driveway while sneaking through the back door of his basement and jumping the fence into a neighbor's yard to go meet with Ramirez, his old partner. Ramirez did the same thing, but borrowed a cousin's car to go pick up Spencer while leaving his car in front of his house, and the light on in his office at home with a mannequin sitting at his desk. Spencer and Ramirez were single guys and no one could account for their whereabouts, except them. The two FBI agents monitoring Ramirez and Spencer were fooled to believe the two of them were home the whole time as they sat in their cars watching the two houses from different locations.

Meanwhile, Martin had a harder time telling his wife he was working overtime that evening. Usually, Officer Nelson would pick up Martin from home in the cruiser. However, Martin asked his wife to drop him off at the station because he had to go to the office to do some paperwork. Before driving directly to the station, Martin suggested to his wife to go food shopping at the supermarket. He wanted to help her, something he had never done in the past. The tagging agent following Martin thought he and his wife were just running their routine errands and didn't feel the need to keep tagging him for the day. He called it into his supervisor and he was given the ok to come to the office. As far as the FBI agent was concerned, Martin was spending personal time with his wife on his day off. The Bureau also called the police station to enquire about Martin's work schedule to confirm it. After food shopping, Mrs. Martin dropped her husband off at the station, and then went on her way. Martin waited until she was out of site before walking down the alley to another street to go meet with Spencer, Ramirez and Nelson who were waiting in a car.

Nelson's exit from his house and away from the FBI surveillance Officer was a little easier. Mrs. Nelson who was a registered nurse often worked a double shift whenever overtime was offered to her. She and Nelson were trying to save some money so they could start planning for a baby. Nelson had a sixteen hour clearance and he didn't have to tell his wife anything about his whereabouts. She was gone. He managed to sneak through his back door and down a back alley to go meet with his Ramirez and Spencer. Like the other two cops, he left a few lights on at the house and music playing to fool the monitoring agents.

The Weakest Link

There was an eerie feeling in the car as the four bandits drove to Connecticut from New York. The conversation among the four crooked cops didn't have the usual flow. Everyone worried that a possible weakest link could be their downfall. Officer Martin didn't offer them any comfort when he kept bringing up the fact that he had to escape from his own house in order to keep the FBI off his tail. "Man, I think it might be a good idea to hire a lawyer and cop a plea before we end up in the electric chair," Martin told his boys while Ramirez kept a steady pace behind the wheel. "The Feds don't have shit and you're getting paranoid for nothing," Ramirez told Martin. "If they don't have shit, why are they tailing us? Why are we even having this conversation then?" Martin asked with his voice cracking. He was really fetching for reassurance that everything was going to be alright. The fear in Martin's voice worried the other three men. "Martin, how much money did you earn last year on the force?" Nelson asked facetiously. "I cleared about sixty thousand last year. Why?" Martin asked. "How much money have you made so far with Little Rob and his crew?" Nelson then asked with sarcasm in his voice. "About seven hundred thousand dollars, but that's not the point,"

Martin said, but before he could finish his thought, Spencer jumped in said, "That is the fucking point. We're out here in the line of fire every fucking day, risking our lives for scumbags like Little Rob and the City thinks our lives are only worth sixty grand after being on the force for almost years. I say we shouldn't feel bad about what we did because these bastards would eventually end up killing each other, anyway." The three officers were trying their best to ease Martin's mind, but he couldn't overcome his worries.

They were now about an hour into the drive. Foxwoods was only about an hour away. The talks continued and no one was really paying attention to the road. Out of the blue, Ramirez asked Martin, Where do you keep all that money in case the Feds come knocking?" Martin was a little hesitant about answering, but he told him he had dug a hole in the backyard of his mother-in-law's house to hide the money. It was easy for him to do that because he helped with the garden every year. She thought he was there trying to get the soil ready for the garden. The guys knew where Martin's mother-in-law lived because they had gone there for cookouts and other family events with Martin. In the midst of the conversation, Martin noticed Ramirez took the wrong exit towards Foxwoods. "What are you doing? This ain't the exit to Foxwoods," he quickly reminded Ramirez. However, it was a little too late because Nelson had already pulled a pistol, placed it on Martin's temple and pulled the trigger. Sitting in the front passenger seat, Spencer turned around to confirm Martin was dead.

The three men didn't really want to kill a fellow officer, but they feared Martin would go to the Feds and start singing like a bird. He was too weak to stay the course and something had to be done about him. Martin's shooting was a mob style murder because he got taken out by a group of people he trusted the most. He never saw it coming. The three officers drove down an abandoned field they had surveyed, dug a hole and placed Martin's body in it. They turned around and drove straight to New York. No one really said much on the drive back. The three officers now made a pact to keep everything they knew to themselves, but they also had some unfinished business in Brooklyn.

Checkmate

Officer Martin's death was being planned from the moment Martin started panicking and raising doubts in their minds after the Feds showed up. All three of the officers, Ramirez, Nelson and Spencer, at some point, had to shoot and kill a rival gang member on the streets for Little Rob to prove their allegiance to the game. When the proposition was made to Martin, he didn't want to go along with it. Killing senselessly was not part of his pedigree. However, because he was already aware the other officers' involvement in Little Rob's operation, they couldn't cut him out. Martin stayed loyal to the team and made illegal arrests just as often as they did. He even planted evidence a few times and whipped some ass every now and then, but he never shot anyone. Though the other officers never allowed Martin to witness any of their killings, he knew whenever someone ended up dead it was on their watch. Martin just knew too much and didn't have the heart and strength to keep his mouth shut. A decision was made by the group to take him out.

Another big event was about to take place in Brooklyn that would change the lives of all the people involved in the Benjamins Click's affairs. Spencer had warned Little Rob to shut down his operations because the Feds were closing in on them. It was an easy decision for Little Rob to consider, since he didn't want his behind to land in prison anyway. Spencer had given him enough time to either shut it down or get taken down with it. "Man, I can't shut down my operation. You know how much money I lost when these stash houses went up in flames? I'm indebted to a lot of people and I need to make this money to get out of debt," Little Rob told Spencer at their meeting under the bridge. "All I'm saying is to shut down the operation, use the money you have already to pay down your debt until shit cools down. I can't control what the Feds do," Spencer warned him. Little Rob was cockier than Spencer ever knew. "Look man, we're gonna move the operation to another spot, but we ain't shutting down. I'm gonna have the Feds believe that we're still at the same spot and let them catch a few stragglers that I need to get rid of anyway, but I got to make this money or it's my ass," Little Rob told him. Spencer had estimated that Little Rob had to bring at least twenty million dollars in cash since the two of them started doing business together. He couldn't understand how Little Rob couldn't pay his debt. I'm just giving you fair warning, because you ain't gonna get no protection from me or my crew when the Feds come knocking," he warned again. "I ain't worried about the Feds. Maybe you and your boys need to start worrying about them. After all, we are partners, partna!" Little Rob told him in a threatening way.

"What the fuck did you say, you little piece of shit!" Spencer had his gun drawn as he approached Little Rob. "You think you can threaten me? What makes you think I won't put a bullet in your ass right now?" Spencer asked rhetorically. "Because my man right here and over there is capturing all this shit on camera, and if I go down, I will take your black ass with me," Little Rob said as he pointed to the two men in the distance over the bridge recording the meeting between Little Rob and Spencer. The two men gave the thumbs up when Spencer looked towards them.

Spencer knew he was cornered, but he couldn't let a street thug like Little Rob think he had the upper hand. He had to act like he would deliver on his threat. He cocked his gun back, placed it against Little Rob's temple while Little Rob's face was pushed against the car window and acted like he was about to shoot. "You think I got anything to lose? Motherfucker, I'll kill every single one of you scumbags and I will get a citation and medal for it," he said angrily. Spencer pushed the gun harder enough against Little Rob's temple to make him understand he was serious and his life was about to become shorter than a breaststroke. While Little Rob screamed in pain from the pressure Spencer was applying with the gun, Spencer took the opportunity to throw an uppercut, hitting Little Rob right on the lips. Blood spewed from Little Rob's mouth. The devious look on Spencer's face was enough to convince Little Rob he was not playing. "You're gonna tell your punk ass boys to throw down their camera, or you're gonna be one dead ass drug dealer," Spencer told him through clinched teeth. In between gasps of breath, Little Rob yelled to his boys to throw their camera over the bridge into the water. "Now, that's how you do it. I'm gonna let you live this time, but if your operation is not shut down by the end of the week, I'm bringing the goon squad for your ass," Spencer told him before hopping in his car and took off.

Since Spencer called Little Rob's bluff, he now had to figure out a way to come up with twenty five million dollars in cash for the Colombia Cartel. Since the burning of the first stash house, Little Rob had been doubling up on his inventory. He lost close to three million dollars in product the first time Kwame burned down his stash house. He pulled the money from his safe to pay off the cartel, leaving him cash strapped, but he was a baller and leader of the crew, he didn't want anybody to know that his money was short. Since Little Rob had been dealing with the cartel for a couple years now, his credit was good with them. In order for him to make up for his loss, he had to increase his supply to meet the demand for the money he owed the cartel. He was on par to make enough money to square up, but Juju got shot. Faced with an already dire situation and a deadline for the cartel to be paid, Little Rob lost an additional twenty million dollars worth of product when the second stash house got burned down. Little

Rob was desperate and he didn't know how or where he was gonna get the money.

Fat Black and Smoov Kev wanted to chill out until things cooled down, but Little Rob wouldn't let them. "Yo, I think we need to chill for a while because popo is gonna be all over our ass after this last hit on us. We got to be smart about this shit. We got enough money to lay low for a while," Fat Black suggested. "I think Fat is right, B. We can't be exposing ourselves like that. You know them mu'fuckas are gunning for us and I ain't trying to get murked before I spend my money," Kev said attempting to make light of the situation. Little Rob wasn't trying to hear it. "You know we lost almost twenty-five mil from the last hit. These mu'fucking Colombians trying to get their paper. They ain't tryna hear we got hit. We gots to keep on pushing to make that money," Little Rob told them. "Yo, these mu'fuckas gotta understand that we got hit. It's part of the game. They gotta give us a little time to square up with them," Fat Black said in frustration. Little Rob looked over at both of them, stared straight into their eyes and said, "Look, I already know y'all ain't got the money for us to pay these mu'fuckas off. Shit, I barely have a million dollars left, 'cause I've had to pay off Juju's debt when the first spot got burned down. I'mma need y'all to stand with me on this or they gonna come for us." This was the first time Little Rob ever showed fear in the face of adversity. He didn't have any other option.

Little Rob was the one who put his crew on and he counted on them to be there for him when he needed them most. He was able to build up enough guilt to force them into agreeing to continue to push forward with the operation, "I thought we were in this together. I brought y'all on because I wanted to make sure we all eat good. But now y'all eating all good and shit, you wanna act like you forgot who put you on. I always been there for y'all and all I'm asking is for y'all to stand with me this time." Little Rob's soliloquy worked. "Come on, B, you know we got you," Smoov Kev said while moving towards Little Rob to dap him. Fat Black got off the couch and moved towards them to create a circle of brotherly love and said, "Come on, man, you know you about the only muthafucka we'd die for." Little Rob got the exact reaction he was looking for. "It's all love," he said, as the three of them were in a group hug.

A Good Feeling

Kwame's last hit brought so much heat, even the mayor was on the news talking about adding extra patrol to the Brownsville area. He knew the last two stash houses were going to be taken down soon by the cops. There was no way the Benjamins Click was gonna keep flying under the radar. It was a matter of time before they got raided. Kwame's mind was at ease and peaceful. He didn't have to worry about Little Rob and his crew anymore bullying the community with their drugs anymore. Their days were numbered.

Kwame spent most of his time renovating the house that he wanted to keep in the family to keep his grandmother's legacy alive. The house was immaculate once Kwame was done with the renovation. The exterior of the house was changed from shingles to stucco. Kwame decided to paint it a light gray with white trims. All new windows were added and a vinyl white fence was erected for privacy. The interior of the house was gutted completely and redesigned to suit the needs of his mother and sister. He laid Brazilian cherry hardwood floors throughout the first floor all the way to the kitchen. New stainless steel appliances were installed, along with new oak cabinets and granite countertop. Janice would never have to wash another dish, because Kwame bought the best stainless steel dishwasher, refrigerator, stove and microwave money could buy. He added a half bath near the kitchen. Kwame opened the walls to give the house an open feel, from the front door all the way to the back door. Upstairs, he tore down all the walls and converted the house from a four-bedroom to a three-bedroom with a full bathroom in each room and a small walk-in closet. The basement was also finished with a full bathroom added and an extra room for guests. The remaining open area in the basement housed Kwame's brand new pool table and entertainment center.

Life was good and Kwame looked forward to the day his mother and sister were returning home. Kwame's last mission netted him a little over two million dollars in cash. He used a portion of the money to renovate his house. The rest of the money went towards the building of a brand new recreation center where the children of Brownsville could participate in different sports, tutoring assistance, drama classes, arts and crafts and peer relation building. The recreation center also served as an afterschool hang out for the children looking for an alternative to the streets. Kwame donated the money his grandmother had left him and his sister for college to the community center to be built in her name, since neither of them attended college. The rest of the money to finish the project was donated anonymously to the Brooklyn borough president who saw the completion of the project. The building got its name from the person Kwame called the biggest inspiration in his life. The Bethune "Grandma" Jones Recreational Center officially opened for business with a ribbon cutting ceremony and welcomed everyone in the neighborhood. Kwame continued to visit with his mother and sister every Sunday. He gave them the option to decide when they felt ready to come home, even though their case managers felt they made great strides toward full recovery. Medicare didn't want to cover the cost beyond the regulated length of time allowed under their policy, but Kwame gladly offered to pay the difference for the additional days that Janice and Jackie stayed at the rehab center.

The Inevitable

Spencer had warned Little Rob to shut down his operation, but he wouldn't listen. Word of a raid got to Spencer and his crew and he made sure he was part of it. The S.W.A.T team was ready and waiting for the captain's order, along with the assisting FBI agents before they rained on the Benjamin Click's parade. Spencer had told Little Rob that the raid would happen within a few days, but it took a little longer for the NYPD and the FBI to orchestrate a raid that would be convenient to both branches of law enforcement. Spencer had to beg his captain to allow him and his team to take part in the raid. He even used Martin's death as a reason to allow him to be a part of the raid. The three cops didn't make it hard for Martin's body to be discovered. They left a big pile of dirt almost as high as a small mountain on the site where Martin's body was buried to make it easy for the cops to find. It was their way of making sure Martin's wife received closure and he be given a proper funeral. An anonymous letter was sent to Martin's wife, telling her about the buried money in his mother in law's backyard. Foul play was always suspected in Martin's death and Little Rob and his crew were the main suspects.

Spencer and his crew had their own reasons for wanting to be part of the raid. Their ulterior motive was kept a secret among them. The captain wanted to reward them for all their hard work in Brownsville. If any officers deserved a citation for cleaning up Brownsville, the captain felt it should've been Spencer's narcotic unit. There wasn't going to be any more warning from Spencer to Little Rob. This time he would be taken down even if Spencer had to do it himself. As the caravan of police cruisers made their way towards Brownsville with sirens blaring, Officer Spencer took the lead. Officer Ramirez and Officer Nelson rode together in another car to the other stash house as the two raids took place simultaneously. The officers had already spoken of their plan. It was a matter of executing it.

The raid at the first house was routine and typical. The NYPD officers outfitted in riot and protective gear shielded themselves behind protective shields as they charged into the house. "Police! Put your hands up!" Spencer yelled as the lead officer inside the house. People were trampling each other as they ran towards windows, doors, bathrooms, rooms, and anything that offered an escape. Naked bodies of women could be seen jumping out of windows, the back door and side doors, but they were surrounded. Spencer knew the money room and knew that he would find Little Rob or Fat Black or even both of them together in that room. His plan was to execute them. He wasn't gonna give either of them a chance to survive. He didn't want them to cut deals with the Feds, implicating Spencer and his men in the process. As Spencer took cover near the back room, he could see movement. He knew there was a person in that back room and they were possibly armed. "Come out with your hands up!" he commanded. The fugitive unloaded a clip from his automatic weapon signifying to the cops, they weren't going to take him alive. The cops scrambled for cover as bullets sprayed throughout the back area of the house. All Spencer wanted was the opportunity to let off one shot to kill whom he was sure was Fat Black. It was a standoff and S.W.A.T Officers were trying their best to talk the perpetrator into giving up. "I ain't going to jail today, buddy," Fat Black said as he unloaded another clip of ammo towards the NYPD officers and FBI agents. Spencer recognized it was Fat Black right away because of his distinctive voice. Fat Black spoke like he was out of breath all the time. Spencer knew he had to make a move to go for the kill once and for all. He signaled for two of the officers to cover him as well as create a diversion by letting off a couple rounds, while he rolled on the floor towards the door on his back. He caught Fat Black against the corner with two shots to his chest. Fat Black died instantly after he was hit.

After securing the rest of the house, the officers emerged with over twenty people in handcuffs. Spencer wondered if Little Rob got away or if he was at the other stash house where Ramirez and Nelson led the raid. He was happy that Fat Black was eliminated. Still, Spencer's mind was not at ease. The last person he wanted to remain alive was Little Rob. Little Rob had been a snitch from the time he met him. He snitched on all the rival gangs and offered information to Spencer to make some of his biggest busts since becoming part of the narcotic unit. Spencer was afraid Little Rob might start talking to save his own ass. He quickly got on the phone to check with Ramirez to make sure everything went as planned. At first, Ramirez didn't pick up his phone because he was still in the middle of the raid. Spencer looked worried and paranoid as he paced back and forth towards his car and back into the stash house, acting like he was trying to make sure the evidence was collected properly. While all the other cops were celebrating a successful raid, Spencer was worried if his enemy #1 had been killed. He waited a few more minutes to call Ramirez once more. Again, Ramirez didn't pick up. Spencer couldn't just leave his crime scene to go check on Ramirez; it would not be the right protocol. Now he was worried more than ever. All kinds of crazy shit started running through his mind. There was shortness of breath as he thought about himself being led in handcuffs to a courtroom where Little Rob is getting ready to get on the stand to testify against him. Spencer was covered in sweat.

The other officers thought he had a hard time coping, because he had just shot a man dead. He played on their ignorance. At their urging, he went to his car to calm himself down. While in his car, Spencer placed a call to Officer Nelson. Nelson picked up, but he was hysterical. "Ramirez is dead, man," were his first words to Spencer. "What do you mean he's dead? What happened?" Spencer asked with shock. "That scumbag, Smoov Kev, shot him in the head," Nelson said while sobbing. Spencer was worried now more than ever. The death of Ramirez didn't necessarily imply the death of Smoov Kev. He wanted to make sure and confirm. "Is Smoov Kev still alive?" he asked with hesitance. "No, he's dead. We unloaded into him," Nelson said without remorse. Spencer felt relieved, knowing that there would be one less witness in court. "What about Little Rob, did you get him?" Spencer asked anxiously. "No, we didn't get him. He wasn't on site," Nelson revealed. Spencer still had a problem and he needed to get to it as soon as possible.

Word of the successful raid spread like wildfire. It was the biggest news of the day on every television station in New York City. Spencer was hailed a hero in the line of fire. The mayor promised to give him a citation for his bravery and valor. "Officer Spencer, were you ever afraid for your life?" one reporter asked him at the scene. Spencer smiled and said, "It's part of the job. It's what I signed up for." That was the only statement he made before jumping into his car to go deal with unfinished business. He never noticed the smirk on the FBI agent's face across the street, after he made his comments on camera. Spencer needed to make sure he got to Little Rob before Little Rob got to the Feds. It was a race against time for Spencer.

Miscalculation

Little Rob was confident that no raid was going to take place because it didn't happen on the day that Spencer warned him it would. The Feds were off by almost a week and it was business as usual for Little Rob and the gang. The Benjamin Click was pushing hard trying to make up the difference they lost in the fire. Little Rob had his people working relentlessly around the clock to ensure delivery of his poison to the community. Smoov Kev and Fat Black were tired from cooking kilos of cocaine into crack during all hours of the night, but a hustler had to hustle. The crew made almost five million dollars in a week, and as a sign of good faith, Little Rob wanted to deliver the money to the Colombian Cartel to buy himself some time. He loaded up his Range Rover with five duffle bags of money and drove down to New Jersey near the shore in Newark, where he met his contact and delivered the money. The man was glad that Little Rob was able to deliver a portion of the money, but he wasn't satisfied. He had to make his position known and Little Rob was roughed up as a result. The beating was nothing as they avoided hitting him on his face. His rib cage, however, was swollen and it was possible that he might've been suffering from internal bleeding. "You have another week to get the twenty million dollars to us, or else it won't be a beating next time," the man in charge told Little Rob before kicking him in the stomach once more, while he was in a fetal position on the ground.

Kwame was glued to the television as the news reported that suspected drug dealer Robert Bailey Jr. evaded cops during a raid at a drug house in Brooklyn. The camera panned for a close-up of Little Rob's mug shot from a past arrest, as the anchor delivered the news of his escape. Kwame had yet to settle his personal vendetta with Little Rob and he felt he may never get the chance. Little Rob received a call from his mother telling him that Smoov Kev and Fat Black were shot and the cops were looking for him. Little Rob was always smart to know that a greater defense was always better than a great offense. He had left over half a million dollars on retainer with his Jewish attorney in Manhattan in case a situation like this ever arose. Little Rob drove straight to the attorney's office to discuss his options and a possible defense to keep him out of jail. He didn't make any mention of Spencer's involvement in his operation to his lawyer. He was holding that information as a last resort. Little Rob walked into the police precinct accompanied with his attorney to turn himself in. He went through the normal procedure of a criminal; got his finger prints done, a mug shot and he was taking to a jail cell until his hearing with one of the judges the next day.

News of Little Rob turning himself in to police got out. Spencer and Nelson were freaking out. They were both afraid that Little Rob only turned himself in to cut a deal. While Nelson was milling over the idea of spending the rest of his life in prison, Spencer was trying to find a way out. However, there was nothing he could do because Little Rob was in protective custody at the precinct located in downtown Brooklyn.

The six o'clock news sought attorney Goldberg for a statement and he gladly offered one. Goldberg was the kind of attorney who lived for the moment and the camera lights couldn't flash any brighter for his career that day. Most of his clients came to know him because of the sensational cases he took on and how he managed to always get his clients the best deals that the state had to offer, and that was only when he couldn't get them off completely. "Mr. Goldberg, do you have a defense prepared for your client?" One reporter asked. Goldberg widened his grin and flashed his crooked smile for the camera and said, "We're gonna have to wait for the wheels of justice to turn because I'm gonna prove my client was a victim of a corrupted system and a victim of extortion." No one knew what to make of Goldberg's statement except two viewing officers who were watching the news in the comfort of their own home, Nelson and Spencer. Officer Nelson definitely felt the pain of the knife stabbing him in his heart when he heard Goldberg's statement. He knew that Little Rob had said something to implicate him. His career was over, his wife was going to leave him and he would lose the respect of his fellow officers, friends and community. He couldn't live with that. Nelson went up to his attic, he pulled out two duffle bags full of money, took them downstairs to his bedroom and left them under the bed for his wife to find.

Mrs. Nelson was at work. Nelson was home alone as he sat on the couch thinking about the possibilities for his life. He had brought shame to his family name. His father was a long time decorated police officer who retired after forty years on the force. He never had a blemish on his record. Officer Nelson couldn't live up to that. He noticed how his father struggled to make ends meet and how his parents argued about money all the time as a child. He didn't want to subject his own family to the same fate. He wanted more for his family, but the NYPD couldn't provide what he wanted. He never thought he was hurting anybody. All he wanted was a better life for his wife and the children they were planning on having, but none of that mattered to him during his last minutes alive. After pouring himself a glass of his favorite scotch, Officer Nelson took his last drink. He pulled out his service revolver, held it under his throat, and fired once. He died instantly from the self-inflicted gunshot wound. Officer Nelson's death was sad, because his wife had planned to surprise him later that evening with the news that they were pregnant. His child would have to grow up without a dad.

Officer Spencer was no coward. He wasn't going out without a fight. After watching the news, he was ready to face whatever fate served him. He went to sleep that evening thinking about his new life in the Caribbean. Those were his new plans. He would escape. However, when he woke up the next day to the news that Officer Nelson had committed suicide, he had to change his plans. He also learned that morning that Little Rob made bail. Kwame saw it on the news as well, and was angry that any judge would allow this scumbag to walk free from a jail cell. Something had to be done and somebody had better do it quick.

An American Hero

The masked man wearing fatigues didn't think twice about walking up to Little Rob to put a gun to his dome in the middle of the street with the sun beaming on him in broad daylight while everybody looked on. He had wanted to do this for months now. He wanted to beat Little Rob at his own game and didn't think about the consequences of how it was done. Word on the street spread like wild fire about the way Little Rob went out like a little bitch. Everybody in the projects had their own version of what took place that day. The actual events that took place became scarier as each witness told a different version of the story. However, the most gruesome version of the story told, was what the folks at Brownsville projects actually wished happened. According to the public information officer of the projects, Ms. Jenkins, who got the best view from the ninth floor in her apartment, a man in Army fatigue wearing a mask walked up to Little Rob just as he was about to hop into his black Rolls Royce that was parked on Sutter Avenue in Brooklyn. Little Rob always felt admired in the projects, so he knew all eyes were always on him whenever he would show up. The bright white colored linen outfit he wore with matching white Prada shoes pulled everyone's attention towards him. The projects were Little Rob's limelight and he basked in it as much as possible. He was a big star who just walked out of jail because he was untouchable. He was the inevitable role model that most black males in the projects didn't need. He flaunted the wealth of the underground world like there was no sinister aspect to it. The fine looking red bone woman sitting in the car waiting for Little Rob only added to the flair of being a hustler. This woman was every project boy's envy and dream. She was one of many to Little Rob, but he never disappointed his young admirers whenever he brought a beautiful thoroughbred to the projects with him. The shiny gloss on her freshly manicured nails was more important to her than her surroundings. She extended one of her hands in front of her looking for any kind of imperfection with her nails. If she found any, Mae Ling would have to see her face again for a do-over, because her gangster boyfriend didn't play that. The tightly fitted white dress she wore barely rested below her thighs as it kept rolling up towards her exposed pussy. Her pussy was well-shaven sans underwear, giving Little Rob a tad bit of pleasurable distraction for his right hand while he drove. As a matter of fact, that was one of his favorite things, having his finger deep inside the moist hole between the legs of a fine woman while he drove around in the hood. Little Rob felt he deserved it because these kept-women were paid for, by him. Nothing was off limits for his women. Rent was always paid on time, car payments were made without questions asked, an endless supply of the latest fad of ghetto jewelry, Gucci, Fendi, Prada and other top designer shoes and handbags were some of the perks for these women. All real shit, too. A finger in their pussy while Little Rob drove was nothing compared to what they were getting. Little Rob was the man. Unfortunately, some of them also never saw the potential stray bullet that could be headed their way while in the company of Little Rob.

Little Rob was on his cell phone using code languages to set up his next deal with his Colombian contact as he casually coasted towards his car. "Little Rob!" the man in dark shades, a black mask, wearing Army fatigues yelled, while pointing his gun towards the back of Little Rob's head. The dumb chick in the car would've had a chance to pull out the .45 Lugar in the glove compartment to help defend her man, Little Rob, only if she wasn't preoccupied with looking over her nails. "Who are you?" Little Rob asked with a little cockiness in his voice. "I'll be asking the questions," the man said as he hit Little Rob in the back of the head with the gun hard enough to create a contusion. Little Rob could feel the swelling on the back of his head, but he was still conscious. Fearing that blood may start pouring over his white linen suit, he asked, "What the fuck do you want, man? Do you know who I am?" Again, he was told, "I'm the man with the gun to your head, and I will be asking all the questions." This time he was hit on the other side of the back of his head. The back of his head now looked like he had two breasts on it. His girlfriend was still busy in the car, now bending down to take inventory of her pedicure. The dark sunglasses on her face made it almost impossible for her to get a clear inspection of her nails, but she continued to try, while her man was getting pistol-whipped with the butt of a gun.

Little Rob still had no clue about the man who was pistol-whipping his ass. The masked man ordered him to keep walking straight towards his car. He was trying to signal to his chick that he was being jacked as he got closer to the car, but she was too dumb to read his signs. The captor moved towards the passenger side of the car and ordered the chick out. "You dumb bitch! I was trying to tell your dumb ass to grab the gun and off this dude, but your dumb ass couldn't get it!" Little Rob said angrily. "You should never refer to a woman as a bitch," the mysterious man said to him, while hitting him with the butt of the gun this time on the forehead. Little Rob was now standing before a mask wearing dude, donned in fatigue, with a loaded gun stuffed Little Rob's mouth and his woman beside him watching the events as they unfolded. By now a mob of onlookers gathered to watch what was happening. "Get on your knees!" the man ordered. Little Rob reluctantly dropped to his knees before pleading, "I got on white threads, bro." The man shook his head, amazed that this fool was worrying more about his clothing than his life. "Get on your crusty ass knees, too, right next to him," he ordered the chick. "And put your hands behind your head," he continued. "Rob, does this muthafucka know who you are? You're dead muthafucka!" she screamed out to the man. Before she could say another word, the man pointed his gun towards Little Rob and unloaded two bullets in each of his knees. "You see these here streets, they are mine and if I ever catch your black ass on this block selling drugs to anybody here, I'm gonna kill you," he told Little Rob before unloading two more bullets into his ankles. Now confined to the ground in agonizing pain, Little Rob was trying to maintain his composure to show the people in the hood that he was a Teflon Don and nobody was going to make him act any less.

The whole ordeal would've been over with, but Little Rob had to make one last stand to show his heart to the people he had been ruling with his drugs for years. As he reached down his ankle faking like he was in pain to grab for his .22 caliber handgun, the masked man turned around and let off four more shots into Little Rob's head, making sure it was his last time breathing. Brain matter splattered all over the ground as his chick lay next to him covered in blood and wondering who that crazy motherfucker was that took out her man in front of everybody in the middle of the day. She definitely was a ride-or-die chick. She reached to grab the gun from Little Rob's hand to exact revenge on the man, but she was met with the barrel of a gun to her head, as the man whispered to her, "Don't even

The Setup

Officer Spencer and his crew of rogue cops had racked up enough money from the Benjamins Click to live comfortably until their calling from God. They couldn't wait for their twenty five years of service date to come up so they could retire in the Caribbean. Their ideology was that they didn't get paid enough by the NYPD to put their lives in jeopardy for nothing. They wanted to live the good life. Never mind the fact that two of them were husbands to two wonderful women, their selfish greed was more important, and took precedence over the livelihood of their family. Life ahead was looking good, as they saw it. The dirty blue code of silence was stronger than it had ever been and all the officers had stashed enough money that would set them financially for life. However, there was always a single shadow lurking. He was none other than the man who had risked his own personal safety and life for the benefit of others. While the officers had ideologies, Kwame had a philosophy. His philosophy was: he had spent six years of his life protecting the lives of Americans in foreign lands all over the world and now the least he could do was to risk his life to protect his own backyard. The officers never saw it coming.

Kwame had been tailing the officers for a while and none of them ever knew it. Spencer had started to get cocky and he thought he was invincible. He had even started to adopt the mentality of a kingpin, untouchable. He didn't seem like he cared that much about his job anymore. Spencer had a habit of leaving the car doors unlocked while it was parked in his driveway at night. Kwame was taking note of his behavior and daily routine. As a matter of fact, he knew where all the officers lived, what time they went to sleep, ate, showered, woke up and left their house everyday. It was so easy to tail these cops, sometimes Kwame would just laugh out loud to himself. The fact that Spencer had started to let his guard down played a big role in his downfall.

Kwame was always one step ahead of him. All of the members of Little Rob's gang were under investigation by the FBI. However, whenever a big bust was scheduled, they were tipped off by Spencer and his boys. The FBI grew suspicious and started an investigation of their own of all the officers of that Narcotic unit. Kwame knew this because he was tailing the FBI while they tailed Spencer and his boys. Initially, two FBI agents were assigned to the case. Whenever the two agents were tailing one cop, Kwame would tail a different member of the Narc unit. Internal Affairs was never notified of the FBI's investigation of Spencer's unit. Spencer thought he was in the clear because he made more arrests than ever before, and confiscated more drugs in Brownsville than any other Narcotic unit from the NYPD. Of course, all the people he was arresting were the rival drug dealers who wanted to set up shop on Little Rob's turf. Their money was short and they couldn't afford to pay what Little Rob's crew was paying Spencer and his boys, and Spencer remained loyal to him.   There was no suspicious sign and the chief of police was happy that order was being restored in Brownsville. There could only be bloodshed and a war if rival gangs are fighting each other, but Little Rob paid the cops and his street informants to make sure no rival gang ever had enough time to establish themselves in Brownsville. Many of the new crews had no idea how the cops were finding out about their operations. Little Rob's hired snitches were always on the prowl looking for information to feed Spencer for a bust. All Little Rob cared about was his money and he did whatever it took to eliminate the competition. However, Juju started creating problems for the Narc Unit when he went on a killing spree.

Til this day, no one really knows who shot Little Rob, the leader of the Benjamins Click. However, the murder weapon was found in a Ziploc bag, along with a face mask, and Army fatigues in the trunk of Officer Spencer's car. Since Officer Spencer was under surveillance twenty-four-hours-a-day, it was hard for the FBI to believe that anybody but Officer Spencer would place these items in his trunk, along with over one hundred thousand dollars in cash hidden in his spare tire. The two FBI agents tailing Officer Spencer never reported to their senior officer that they drove down to Dunkin Donuts to grab coffee and donuts, which was an open opportunity for evidence to be planted.

When a tip was received at FBI headquarters via a phone call from a private number about a black Crown Victoria in Brooklyn under a bridge where a person appeared to be changing his clothes and also pulled out a stack of money from around his waist and placed it under the spare tire in the trunk of the car, the commanding Officer from FBI headquarters ordered the arrest of Officer Spencer. Picture and video proofs of meetings between Little Rob and Officer Spencer, showing money exchanges were also delivered to FBI headquarters via FedEx. There were about twenty people willing to testify that the person who shot Little Rob was about the same height and same build as Officer Spencer. The FBI had a tight case. However, the most damning evidence was the phone call Spencer made to Officer Nelson while he was in his car. The FBI had planted a tapping device in Officer Spencer's car.

Que Sera, Sera

The battle was won, but the war continue in every black neighborhood in America as more people fall victim to the lure of fast money and drug addiction everyday. It was time for Kwame to take a break and reconnect with the love of his life. After setting up his mother and sister in the house after they came home from rehab, Kwame took them shopping for new clothes, paid to get their hair done and took them out to dinner to celebrate. He even paid to get Jackie's teeth whitened. Kwame had never talked about the death of his father with his mom up to this point. While catching up at dinner, the topic came up in conversation. Jackie was especially thrilled to hear about the father she never got to know. As Janice started to explain to her kids the life their father had dreamed up for them, she couldn't help getting emotional. Jackie and Kwame could see the love that still existed in their mother's heart for their father. She also smiled when she brought up the good memories they shared. Kwame and his sister were proud to know that their father was a great man. Janice felt especially lucky that her son came home just in time to save her life.

The conversation would end sadly when Janice started talking about the events that led up to their father's death. Janice had never mentioned the name of the man who shot and killed their dad throughout their entire lives. However, when she finally told them the man's name was Robert Bailey, a smirk ran across the faces of Kwame and Jackie, because the man reported shot on the news a couple of days prior was named Robert Bailey, Jr., AKA Little Rob, the son of Robert Bailey, AKA Black Rob. Kwame told his mother and sister how he was falling for Sandrine and he wanted them to meet her. Also, she was coming to spend a couple of weeks with him at the house.

Kwame made the arrangements for Sandrine to fly from Paris to New York. He was excited. It was time to take his relationship with her to the next level. They had missed each other so much. They couldn't keep their hands off each other when Sandrine finally got to New York. Sandrine also connected right away with Janice and Jackie. She even reminded Janice of her youth. Sandrine loved New York and hoped to one day move closer to Kwame so they can explore the endless possibilities of their relationship.

Kwame was very realistic in his thinking. Though he loved Sandrine and dreamed of one day having a family with her, he also thought about all the other neighborhoods across America that have to deal with people like Little Rob, Officer Spencer and the other ghetto bastards that refuse to allow any kind of upward mobility in the ghetto. He was seriously considering making "cleaning up the ghetto" his life's

- 244 -

journey. You never know, he may show up in your run-down town one day to help with the clean-up.

The End

Sample chapters from King Of Detroit

Chapter One

-1987-

I remember the last time I saw my father alive, that day will forever be stuck in my memory. We were sitting at a red light on 7 Mile and Conant with the top down on my Pops new triple black Benz. We were listening to Frankie Beverly and Mayes, sounds pumpin', when out of nowhere a black van rammed us from behind. An old silver Chrysler pulled on the driver's side and tried boxing us in, but just as two masked gunmen exited the van, the light turned green and Pops smashed out, jumping the curb and making a hard right turn down Conant.

"Get down!" King David yelled, pushing me down.

The gunmen let off a few shots, one hitting the dashboard and another cracking the windshield. Pops lifted the top on the Benz while plotting our escape route. Seeing that the Chrysler was only a few cars behind and the van not too far behind them, Pops smashed the gas trying to get enough distance to make a turn down a side street.

"Son listen, I am going to turn this next corner, and when I do, I want you to jump out," Pops said scanning the rearview mirror.

"I'm not leaving you," I said. My heart was racing.

"Coach, now isn't the time. I am not about to chance letting anything happen to you." Pops bent the corner doing damn near fifty, he slammed on the brakes and came to a violent stop. "Go! Go!" he yelled.

"I don't want to," I said refusing to get out of the car.

"Coach, get the fuck out of the car now!" he yelled. Pops reached over to open my door and pushed me out of the car. I landed on my side and by this time the old Chrysler and black van were bending the corner.

"Run Coach!" yelled Pops.

I hesitated because I didn't want to leave my father. Although there wasn't much I could do besides die beside him, I was willing to do that.

"Got damn it Coach, run!" Pops yelled while looking back. I reluctantly got up, turned and started running. It was too late, the Chrysler had boxed Pops in and the gunmen in the van were out, guns drawn. I stopped at the corner and hid behind some bushes as I watched the men snatch Pops out of the car and drag him to the van at gun point. They threw him in the back, then sped off with the Chrysler in tow.

That was the last time I saw my father alive. And I have to live with the fact that I cost him his life by hesitating. If I had followed his instructions and just ran he would have had enough time to get away as well.

*****

"You peon muthafuckas think ya'll gone get away with snatchin' me. Do you know who the fuck I am?"

"Yeah, a dead man," one of the masked gunmen jokingly said.

"Mothafucka, I'm King David!"

"Yeah, and I'm King Tut. Why don't you just shut the fuck up and accept the fact that yo' ass 'bouts to die."

The black van pulled into the driveway of an abandoned two- family flat on the east side of Detroit. The van stopped at the side door of the house and one of the gunmen slid the door open on the van.

"Ya'll ready for this bitch?" he asked.

"Yeah, bring his ass down in the basement," a man standing in the doorway demanded.

"Come on bitch, show time."

Two gunmen snatched King David up and escorted him into the house and down into the basement. It was pitch dark down there the only light was the sun rays peeking through the dusty windows. It smelled like death

down there. Needles, empty beer cans, dirty soiled
mattresses, clothes, etc. cluttered the basement giving it a
musty smell. The gunmen escorted King David to a
wooden chair and pushed him down in it.

"Tie his ass up," one man ordered.

Two masked men immediately began wrapping rope around
KD's skinny frame.

"You lollypop ass nuccas really think ya'll gone get away
with this. As soon as my man finds out I'm missin' the city
will be shut down," KD snapped confidently.

"And who is your man?" asked one of the masked men.

"I'm certain you've heard of him, Dump."

"Dump? You hear this old clown nucca. He thinks Dump
is going to save him." Everyone started laughing.

"So you think Dump is going to save you, huh?" asked the
masked man, as he peeled off his mask, which had been
muffling his voice.

King David's eyes damn near popped out his heart at the
sight standing before him. His entire body was filled with
rage and disbelief. He couldn't believe what he was seeing.
It was his right hand man, Dump. The very man he thought
was going to save his life.

"Why Dump?" asked King David.

"Question is, why not?" Your time is over, been over but your bitch ass refused to pass the torch so, I'm taking it."

"What do you want" asked King David.

"What I have always wanted for you to see me as the king. I could have just had them kill you but I needed for you to know who dethroned you."

"So, what's next Dump?"

"For you to call me King."

"I will never call you King. You are a snake and I fault myself for not seeing this coming."

"Oh, you will call me 'King Dump' one way or another. We're going to start with your fingers, one by one we're going to chop 'em off. And then we'll work on the toes and so forth. But you will honor me before you die. Grab that saw and bring it over here," ordered Dump.

One of his flunkies quickly retrieved the power saw and handed it over to Dump. The saw made a violent screeching sound as it came to life.

"You hear that?" Dump asked while squeezing the saw's trigger. "Now tell me, what's my name?" he asked while lowering the saw to King David's right foot.

"Clown," King David answered.

"Wrong answer," Dump said, then pressed the spinning blade against the bone of King David's big toe. Blood shot everywhere as Dump forced the blade through.

"Ahh…" screamed King David in agony. His big toe now sat in front of him, the bone could be seen where it was disconnected, and blood continued to spurt in all directions.

"Just think, only nine more to go," Dump taunted.

"Now let's try again. What' my name?"

"Coward!" yelled King David, as he spit in Dump's face.

"Pull his pants down," ordered Dump. "Pull 'em all the way down, his boxers too."

"What you gone do now, such my dick" snapped King David as he sat there exposed for all to see.

"Nah, bitch. Keith grab his dick and hold it up."

"What?" Keith asked in disbelief, not wanting to touch another man's dick.

"Just do what the fuck I said," yelled Dump. He was getting frustrated. All he wanted was the respect of the streets. He had managed to turn Keith and a few other workers under him against King David. Keith reluctantly grabbed a hold of King David's manhood and tried not to make eye contact with him.

"That's right Keith, do as you're told. I knew you were a spineless snake coward bitch nucca. I should have killed…"

The sound of the saw and sudden pain cut King David's sentence short. I mean literally cut it short. He was in so much pain that all he could do is hope for death. Dump held King David's dick in his hand, which was now detached. He held it up in the air, then said, "You are no longer a man. You are a bitch to the highest power," he said then burst out into a sinister laugh.

Dump slapped King David hard across the face with his own dick. "You may never call me King, but your son lil' Coach, I will definitely be his King. Finish this bitch off," Dump ordered as he handed the saw to Keith.

Just like that, Dump crowned himself the new King. He had laid and laid for his opportunity to take over and today was that day. He exited the basement as King Dump, while his best friend and boss screamed in severe agony as Keith and the gang finished torturing him. They cut all his toes and fingers off, and severed his head, arms and legs. Dump left orders to box up King David's body parts and have them delivered to the streets in broad daylight. Dump wanted to send a clear message that he was the new King.

Chapter Two

I ran full speed back up to 7 Mile and Conant to Church's Chick on the corner. I picked up the pay phone and tried calling home but the phone just rang and rang. "Come on pick up," I said as the voicemail picked up for the fifth time. I slammed the phone down, angry with tears in my eyes from not knowing what to do. I took a deep breath and pulled myself together, now was not the time to be folding, King David needed me. I scanned the parking lot and spotted a Checker cab, startling the Arab driver as I banged on the driver side window. He cracked the window just enough to speak, "Yes, can I help you?"

"Can you take me to Caldwell Street?" I asked.

"Do you have money?" the cab driver asked.

I pulled out two crispy twenties and watched as the driver's eyes lit up. He turned the key starting the cab. "Get in. Get in, I drive you."

We lived about twenty miles from Church's Chicken and the cab driver was trying to run up the meter driving slow as shit. We must've gotten caught by every light on 7 Mile. As we pulled onto my street, I could see a lot of cars down near my house and the street was blocked off making it impossible for us to get down the street. I gave the driver both twenties and then jumped out, "Thanks." I ran full speed non-stop all the way to my house. Police cars and yellow tape from the crime unit had my house blocked off. I tried crossing the tape when a young officer grabbed my arm. "Where do you think you're going young man?"

"I live here. That's my house," I said trying to move past the officer, but he had a firm grip.

"Just calm down and let me try and locate the owner, but you cannot pass this tape, it's a crime scene."

I could see a large brown box with blood stains sitting in our front lawn but I didn't pay it much attention 'cause I was desperately trying to locate my mother, so I could let her know about my dad. A few moments later I saw my mother being escorted to a squad car by a female officer. My mom was hysterical, she was screaming and crying at the top of her lungs.

"Ma!" I yelled out.

The officer took his eyes off me for a brief second, which was all I needed. I bolted towards my mom full speed. She turned to face me then met me half way with open arms.

"Corey, baby, are you okay?" she asked a bit relieved after examining me from head to toe. My dad and I had just left the house, we left together so Ma was concerned.

"Ma, they took dad," I said softly.

"I know baby," she said crying then pulled me close to her.

"I know," she sobbed.

"Is he okay, where is he Ma?" I asked.

"No. Why?" Mom screamed. She went back into a trance. I thought she was having a nervous breakdown out there. She fell to both knees and kept banging on the ground cursing God, asking "Why?"

A female officer helped mom up to her feet and carefully escorted her to an awaiting squad car. I felt absolutely helpless as I watched my mom breakdown. I had never seen her cry a day before in my life.

My mom was the most beautiful woman you'd ever meet. I mean inside and out. Moms was a petite red bone with short black wavy hair, who stayed laced in nothing but the best, courtesy of Pops, King David. She was in her early 30's and had this I'm young forever attitude. She wouldn't let me call her Ma too often, she said it made her feel old. We was on some first name basis shit. She made me and all my friends call her by her government, Tina. But Ma Dukes was my dawg, she always had my back and treated me like a brother rather than a son.

When I was 10, she started letting me hit the weed with her. She said she'd rather I smoke with her at home than to be out getting high doing some bullshit. We just had that relationship most nuccas wish they had with their

Moms. Moms was a rider too. She bust her gun and was a

natural born hustla, which is why King David nabbed her in

the first place. It was Ma Dukes who introduced King David

to his coke and heroin connect in Cali, which is where Ma

Dukes is originally from. Pops was out in Cali looking for

some work back in the 70's when he met Ma Dukes at a

strip club. Ma Dukes used to strip back in the day and I

guess she put that pussy on Pops just right 'cause when he

left Cali, he took Moms back to Detroit with him, her and

two bricks of work. They been on some Bonnie and Clyde

shit every since. They had me a few years later, I'm the only

child.

*****

I'm standing there in our front lawn watching all the

movement, when I see a crime unit open that brown box and

start taking pictures from different angles. I saw what

appeared to be an arm, and my stomach touched my ass as I

feared the worst. I looked closer and swallowed hard, not

wanting to accept what my eyes were seeing. It was an arm,

that of my father. I knew it was him by the distinct tattoo he

had on his forearm, which read 'King David' with two

arrows on each end, one facing up and the other one down.

The arrows symbolized the game. King David said that 'the

same nuccas you see at the top will be the same nuccas you see at the bottom.' Each time I thought about that metaphor it meant something different every time.

This can't be, I told myself. My daddy, was a warrior, he didn't go out that easy. But there was no denying it I knew that tattoo from anywhere and the light brown skin of King David's, which was identical to mine. I couldn't hold my stomach from the sight, my knees buckled as I threw up everything that I had eaten in the past two days. My best friend Rocko slid past the tape and rushed to my side. "Coach man get up," he said trying to pull me to my feet. But I was still throwing up my guts. "Come on Coach, I got you man." Rocko was my dawg for real. We had been best friends since birth. We were the same age and our birthdays were only two days apart, mine on the 26th of February and his on the 28th. Growing up we always celebrated our birthdays together. All the girls in school thought we were brothers because we somewhat favored both standing at 5'10" and weighed about 160 pounds soak and wet. Rocko was a little darker than me though, but other than that we could definitely pass for brothers. We both wore our hair in low bald fades with the pencil waves courtesy of 'Murray's' grease.

King David and Rocko's dad, Dump, were stick-men. They had the same relationship Rocko and I had, when you saw one the other one wasn't too far away, which is why I couldn't understand how something like this could happen and to my dad, he was King David. They had just snatched him not even two hours ago, and yet he beat me home in a box. "Where was everybody when all this was going on?" I asked myself.

We lived dead center on the block in a ridiculously renovated house with about ten additions and four extra garages. King David owned the entire street both sides of the block and four houses were fenced in together with ours in the middle. A Pit-bull farm was out back with at least thirty dogs. We had modern security surveillance cameras posted throughout the block and our house, not to mention all the workers on the block who were holding heat. Then on the opposite side of the street, Dump had a similar setup with his house sitting directly across from ours. So I couldn't understand how nuccas would feel comfortable enough to hit the block and leave a box with King David in it. I could hear the husky voice of Dump nearing as I sat on my knees still pucking.

"Let me through, this is my brother's house!" Dump demanded.

"Dad, over here!" yelled Rocko.

"They killed KD, dad. Somebody pulled up and sat this box on the grass and peeled off," Rocko said giving Dump a brief run down.

"I know son," Dump softly said. He kneeled down and picked me up and pulled me close to his large frame. He hugged me tight and rubbed my head as if I were his very own son. "I swear to you Coach I'm going to find who did this. That I promise you. You know unck has never lied to you, right?" Dump asked now crying his heart out.

"They killed my daddy." I sobbed into Dump's chest.

"It's gone be alright. Unck, is going to handle everything. Come on let's go across the street."

We walked across the street to Dump's crib where now everybody was gathered. I couldn't help but think, where were all you nosy muthafuckas when them nuccas threw my daddy's body out here.

"It's gone be alright Coach, baby. Auntie is here for you," Kathy said while rocking me back and forth in her arms on the sofa. We were all seated in the front room, nobody saying much with the exception of Dump. He paced back and forth barking orders into the cordless phone he held. "I want every nucca on the block suited and fuckin' booted in ten minutes!" he said, then slammed the phone down on the glass coffee table. "Kathy, take Coach in the back and wash him up," Dump ordered.

Kathy was Dump's latest broad he was fuckin' and sponsoring. She was at least twenty years younger than him and the only reason she was dealing with Dump was on the strength of his money. Kathy was a bad little bitch; chocolate skin, long black silky hair, tight stomach, fat ass, big titties and a pretty face. She was your typical bad hood bitch who had fallen on hard times and was looking for the highest bidder to take care of her ass.

Dump stood 6'8" and weighed every bit of 350 pounds. He was not at all in shape, his stomach protruded over his pants, he had rolls on his back and neck, and his hygiene was never on point. Dump was black as they came and ugly as hell. God must have been in a bad mood when he made Dump, cause his ass was not a sight you'd want to see. Rocko really lucked out not receiving Dump's genes. I guess he took after his Moms, but I never met Rocko's old bird, she supposedly died in a car accident when we were babies. Dump got his name cause coming up he was known for killin' nuccas and dumping their bodies in the river over the Belle Isle Bridge. He was King David's right hand and under boss. They grew up in the very houses that they lived in and been friends like Rocko and I since day one.

"Come on Coach let me run your bath," Kathy said pulling me up from the sofa.

I was like a zombie. I didn't care nothing about taking no bath, but I was too drained to argue, so I reluctantly followed Kathy into the back and into the bathroom. Kathy closed the door behind me and locked it, then started running the water. She began removing my clothes starting with my shirt and then pants. "Don't be shy now Coach, take off your drawers, the water is almost ready," she said.

I was only twelve at the time but I knew all about pussy. King David used to pay strippers to suck my dick and to fuck me. I was too young to bust a nut, but I was gettin' it in and my lil' dick would rock up in a minute. I had my eye on Kathy's lil' ass since Dump started fuckin' with her and she would always playfully flirt with me and Rocko, telling us we were scared of pussy.

"I'm gone get in with you," she said dropping her silk house robe to the floor. She was ass naked and smelled like a fresh rose. She seductively climbed into the whirlpool style tub and dipped her entire body into the water, then stood up covered in soap suds. "You comin' Coach, Dump told me to wash you up," she said softly. "Why you shy? I'll turn my head," she said, then turned and started messing with the radio. Keith Sweat's crying ass came pouring out of the speakers. I quickly pulled down my boxer shorts and stepped out of them, as I lifted my head Kathy was staring right at my shit. "Hmm. How old are you Coach?" she asked jokingly.

I wasn't at all ashamed of my blessing 'cause for my age I was well developed. I climbed in the tub a little tensed, as Kathy noticed.

"Relax Coach," she said pulling me towards her, then turning me around. I sat between her legs while she softly scrubbed my back with a sponge, then reached around and washed my chest.

I'm laying there with my back against her chest with my eyes closed head to the ceiling, thinking about all that has happened. Kathy wrapped her thick legs around my waist and rubbed her soft fingers across my face. She whispered in my ear sincerely "You're the next King, Coach."

Serosa becomes the subject to information that could financially ruin and possibly destroy the lives and careers of many prominent people involved in the government if this data is exposed. As this intricate plot thickens, speculations start mounting and a whirlwind of death, deceit, and betrayal finds its way into the ranks of a once impenetrable core of the government. Will Serosa fall victim to the genetic structure that indirectly binds her to her parents causing her to realize there s NO WAY OUT!

In Stores!!!

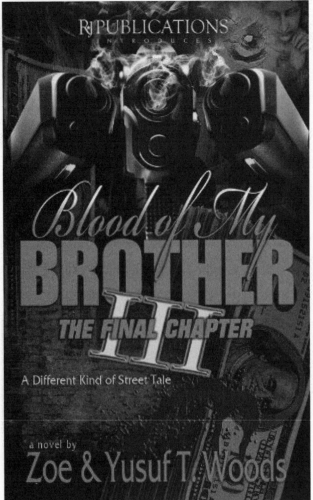

Retiring is no longer an option for Roc, who is now forced to restudy Philly's vicious streets through blood filled eyes. He realizes that his brother's killer is none other than his mentor, Mr. Holmes. With this knowledge, the strategic game of chess that began with the pushing of a pawn in the Blood of My Brother series, symbolizes one of love, loyalty, blood, mayhem, and death. In the end, the streets of Philadelphia will never be the same...

In Storess!!!

After Chasin' Satisfaction, Julius finds that satisfaction is not all that it's cracked up to be. It left nothing but death in its aftermath. Now living the glamorous life in Miami while putting the finishing touches on his hybrid condo hotel, he realizes with newfound success he's now become the hunted. Julian's success is threatened as someone from his past vows revenge on him.

In Stores!!!

It may not be Histeria Lane, but these desperate housewives are fed up with their neglecting husbands. Their sexual needs take precedence over the millions of dollars their husbands bring home every year to keep them happy in their affluent neighborhood. While their husbands claim to be hard at work, these wives are doing a little work of their own with the bedroom bandit. Is the bandit swift enough to evade these angry husbands?

In Stores!!

NEGLECTED SOULS

Motherhood and the trials of loving too hard and not enough frame this story...The realism of these characters will bring tears to your spirit as you discover the hero in the villain you never saw coming...

In Stores!!!

Jimmy and Nina continue to feel a void in their lives because they haven't a clue about their genealogical make-up. Jimmy falls victims to a life threatening illness and only the right organ donor can save his life. Will the donor be the bridge to reconnect Jimmy and Nina to their biological family? Will Nina be the strength for her brother in his time of need? Will they ever find out what really happened to their mother?

In Stores!!!

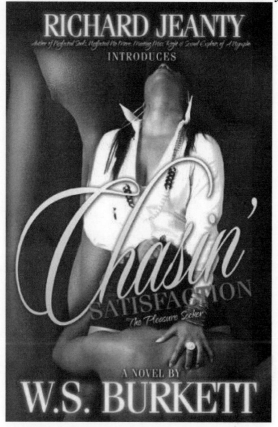

Betrayal, lust, lies, murder, deception, sex and tainted love frame this story... Julian Stevens lacks the ambition and freak ability that Miko looks for in a man, but she married him despite his flaws to spite an ex-boyfriend. When Miko least expects it, the old boyfriend shows up and ready to sweep her off her feet again. She wants to have her cake and eat it too. While Miko's doing her own thing, Julian is determined to become everything Miko ever wanted in a man and more, but will he go to extreme lengths to prove he's worthy of Miko's love? Julian Stevens soon finds out that he's capable of being more than he could ever imagine as he embarks on a journey that will change his life forever.

In Stores!!!

The police in New York and other major cities around the country are increasingly victimizing black men. The violence has escalated to deadly force, most of the time without justification. In this controversial book, noted author Richard Jeanty, tackles the problem of police brutality and the unfair treatment of Black men at the hands of police in New York City and the rest of the country.

In Stores!!!

Just when Darren thinks his relationship with Tina is flourishing, there is yet another hurdle on the road hindering their bliss. Tina saw a therapist for months to deal with her sexual addiction, but now Darren is wondering if she was ever treated completely. Darren has not been taking care of home and Tina's frustrated and agrees to a break-up with Darren. Will Darren lose Tina for good? Will Tina ever realize that Darren is the best man for her?

In Stores!!

Ronald Murphy was a player all his life until he and his best friend, Myles, met the women of their dreams during a brief vacation in South Beach, Florida. Sexual Jeopardy is story of trust, betrayal, forgiveness, friendship and hope.

In Stores!!!

Tina develops an insatiable sexual appetite very early in life. She only loves her boyfriend, Darren, but he's too far away in college to satisfy her sexual needs.

Tina decides to get buck wild away in college

Will her sexual trysts jeopardize the lives of the men in her life?

In Stores!!!

Faith Jones, a woman in her mid-thirties, has given up on ever finding love again until she met her son's best friend, Darius. Faith Jones is walking a thin line of betrayal against her son for the love of Darius. Will Faith allow her emotions to outweigh her common sense?

In Stores!!!

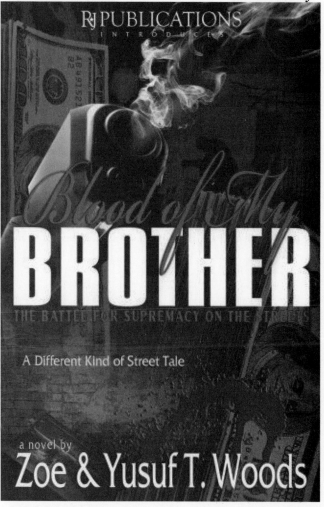

Roc was the man on the streets of Philadelphia, until his younger brother decided it was time to become his own man by wreaking havoc on Roc's crew without any regards for the blood relation they share. Drug, murder, mayhem and the pursuit of happiness can lead to deadly consequences. This story can only be told by a person who has lived it.

In Stores!!!

Violence, Intimidation and carnage are the order as Nathan and his brother set out to build the most powerful drug empires in Chicago. However, when God comes knocking, Nathan's conscience starts to surface. Will his haunted criminal past get the best of him?

In Stores!!

RJ PUBLICATIONS
I N T R O D U C E S

Stick & MOVE

A Different Kind of Street Tale

a novel by
SHAWN BLACK

Yasmina witnessed the brutal murder of her parents at a young age at the hand of a drug dealer. This event stained her mind and upbringing as a result. Will Yamina's life come full circle with her past? Find out as Yasmina's crew, The Platinum Chicks, set out to make a name for themselves on the street.

In stores!!

Ashland's mother, Bianca, fights hard to suppress the truth from her daughter because she doesn't want her to marry Jordan, the grandson of an ex-lover she loathes. Ashland soon finds out how cruel and vengeful her mother can be, but what price will Bianca pay for redemption?

In stores!!

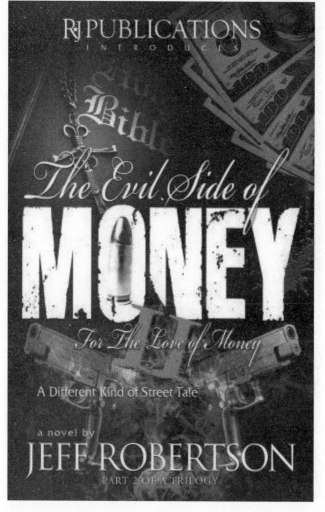

A beautigul woman from Bolivia threatens the existence of the drug empire that Nate and G have built. While Nate is head over heels for her, G can see right through her. As she brings on more conflict between the crew, G sets out to show Nate exactly who she is before she brings about their demise.

In Stores!!!

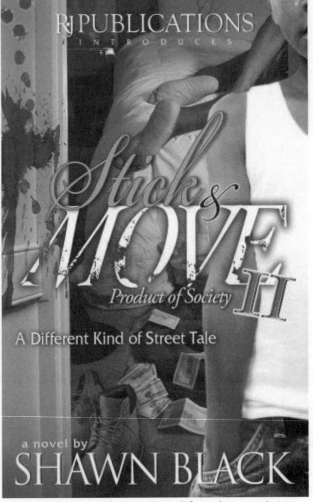

Scorcher and Yasmina's low key lifestyle was interrupted when they were taken down by the Feds, but their daughter, Serosa, was left to be raised by the foster care system. Will Serosa become a product of her environment or will she rise above it all? Her bloodline is undeniable, but will she be able to control it?

In Stores!!

An ex-drug dealer finds himself in a bind after he's caught by the Feds. He has to decide which is more important, his family or his loyalty to the game. As he fights hard to make a decision, those who helped him to the top fear the worse from him. Will he get the chance to tell the govt. whole story, or will someone get to him before he becomes a snitch?

In Stores!!!

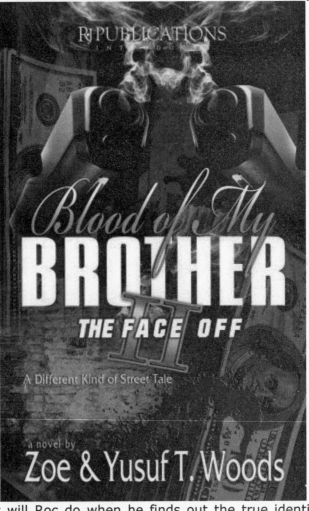

What will Roc do when he finds out the true identity of Solo? Will the blood shed come from his own brother Lil Mac? Will Roc and Solo take their beef to an explosive height on the street? Find out as Zoe and Yusuf bring the second installment to their hot street joint, Blood of My Brother.

In Stores!!!

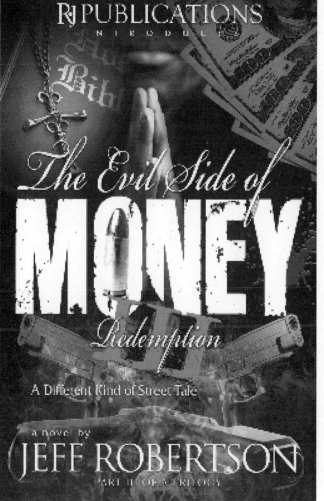

Forced to abandon the drug world for good, Nathan and G attempt to change their lives and move forward, but will their past come back to haunt them? This final installment will leave you speechless.

In Stores!!!

Nafiys Muhammad managed to beat the charges in court and was found innocent as a result. However, his criminal involvement is far from over. While Jerry Class Classon is feeling safe in the witness protection program, his family continues to endure even more pain. There will be many revelations as betrayal, sex scandal, corruption, and murder shape this story. No one will be left unscathed and everyone will pay the price for his/her involvement. Get ready for a rough ride as we revisit the Black Top Crew.

In Stores!!

Dave Richardson is enjoying success as his second book became a New York Times best-seller. He left the life of The Bedroom behind to settle with his family, but an obsessed fan has not had enough of Dave and she will go to great length to get a piece of him. How far will a woman go to get a man that doesn't belong to her?

In Stores!!!

Deon is at the mercy of a ruthless gang that kidnapped him. In a foreign land where he knows nothing about the culture, he has to use his survival instincts and his wit to outsmart his captors. Will the Hoodfellas show up in time to rescue Deon, or will Crazy D take over once again and fight an all out war by himself?

In Stores!!!

The drama continues as Deshun is hunted by Angela who still feels that ex-girlfriend Kayla is still trying to win his heart, though he brutally raped her. Angela will kill anyone who gets in her way, but is DeShun worth all the aggravation?

In Stores!!!

Buck Johnson was forced to make the best out of worst situation. He has witnessed the most cruel events in his life and it is those events who the man that he has become. Was the Johnson family ignorant souls through no fault of their own?

In Stores!!!

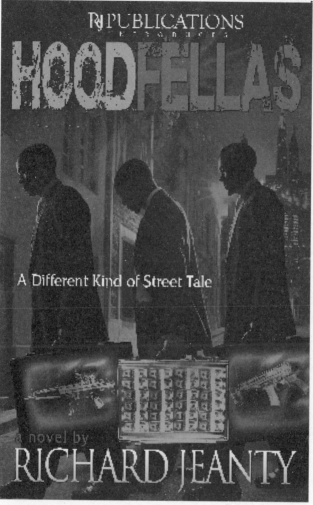

When an Ex-con finds himself destitute and in dire need of the basic necessities after he's released from prison, he turns to what he knows best, crime, but at what cost? Extortion, murder and mayhem drives him back to the top, but will he stay there?

In Stores !!!

What happens when someone falls insanely in love? Stalking is just the beginning.

In Stores!!!

Pharaoh decides that his fate would not be settled in court by twelve jurors. His fate would be decided in blood, as he sets out to kill Tez, and those who snitched on him. Pharaoh s definition of Going All Out is either death or freedom. Prison is not an option. Will Pharoah impose his will on those snitches?

In Stores 10/30/2011

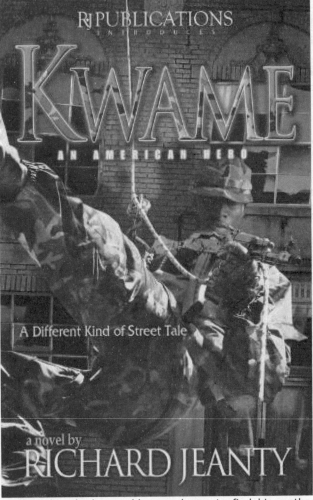

Kwame never thought he would come home to find his mother and sister strung out on drugs after his second tour of duty in Iraq. The Gulf war made him tougher, more tenacious, and most of all, turned him to a Navy Seal. Now a veteran, Kwame wanted to come back home to lead a normal life. However, Dirty cops and politicians alike refuse to clean the streets of Newark, New Jersey because the drug industry is big business that keeps their pockets fat. Kwame is determined to rid his neighborhood of all the bad elements, including the dirty cops, dirty politicians and the drug dealers. Will his one-man army be enough for the job?

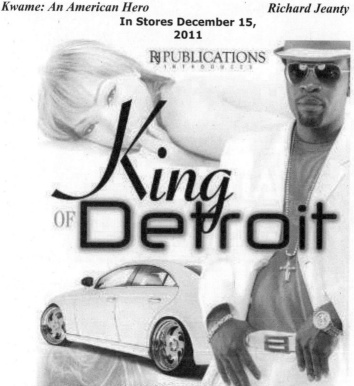

In Stores December 15, 2011

RJ PUBLICATIONS
INTRODUCES

King OF Detroit

A Different Kind of Street Tale

a novel by
DORIAN SYKES

The blood-thirsty streets of Detroit have never seen a King like Corey Coach Townsend. The Legacy of Corey Coach Townsend, the Real King of Detroit, will live on forever. Coach was crowned King after avenging his father s murder, and after going to war with his best friend over the top spot. He always keeps his friends close. Coach s reign as king will forever be stained in the streets of Detroit, as the best who had ever done it, but how will he rise to the top? This is a story of betrayal, revenge and honor. There can only be one king!

In Stores February 15, 2012

PUBLICATIONS
BRINGING EXCITEMENT, FUN AND JOY TO READING

Use this coupon to order by mail

1. Neglected Souls, Richard Jeanty $14.95 Available
2. Neglected No More, Richard Jeanty $14.95 Available
3. Ignorant Souls, Richard Jeanty $15.00, Available
4. Sexual Exploits of Nympho, Richard Jeanty $14.95 Available
5. Meeting Ms. Right's Whip Appeal, Richard Jeanty $14.95 Available
6. Me and Mrs. Jones, K.M Thompson $14.95 Available
7. Chasin' Satisfaction, W.S Burkett $14.95 Available
8. Extreme Circumstances, Cereka Cook $14.95 Available
9. The Most Dangerous Gang In America, R. Jeanty $15.00 Available
10. Sexual Exploits of a Nympho II, Richard Jeanty $15.00 Available
11. Sexual Jeopardy, Richard Jeanty $14.95 Available
12. Too Many Secrets, Too Many Lies, Sonya Sparks $15.00 Available
13. Stick And Move, Shawn Black $15.00 Available
14. Evil Side Of Money, Jeff Robertson $15.00 Available
15. Evil Side Of Money II, Jeff Robertson $15.00 Available
16. Evil Side Of Money III, Jeff Robertson $15.00 Available
17. Flippin' The Game, Alethea and M. Ramzee, $15.00 Available
18. Flippin' The Game II, Alethea and M. Ramzee, $15.00 Available
19. Cater To Her, W.S Burkett $15.00 Available
20. Blood of My Brother I, Zoe & Yusuf Woods $15.00 Available
21. Blood of my Brother II, Zoe & Ysuf Woods $15.00 Available
22. Hoodfellas, Richard Jeanty $15.00 available
23. Hoodfellas II, Richard Jeanty, $15.00 03/30/2010
24. The Bedroom Bandit, Richard Jeanty $15.00 Available
25. Mr. Erotica, Richard Jeanty, $15.00, Sept 2010
26. Stick N Move II, Shawn Black $15.00 Available
27. Stick N Move III, Shawn Black $15.00 Available
28. Miami Noire, W.S. Burkett $15.00 Available
29. Insanely In Love, Cereka Cook $15.00 Available
30. Blood of My Brother III, Zoe & Yusuf Woods Available
31. Mr. Erotica
32. My Partner's Wife
33. Deceived I
34. Deceived II
35. Going All Out I
36. Going All Out II 10/30/2011
37. Kwame 12/15/2011
38. King of Detroit 2/15/2012

Name_____

Address_____

City_____State_____Zip Code_____

Please send the novels that I have circled above.
Shipping and Handling: Free
Total Number of Books_____Total Amount Due_____
            Buy 3 books and get 1 free. Send institution check or money order (no cash or
CODs) to: RJ Publication: PO Box 300771, Jamaica, NY 11434
For info. call 718-471-2926, or www.rjpublications.com allow 2-3 weeks for delivery.

Use this coupon to order by mail

39. Neglected Souls, Richard Jeanty $14.95 Available
40. Neglected No More, Richard Jeanty $14.95 Available
41. Ignorant Souls, Richard Jeanty $15.00, Available
42. Sexual Exploits of Nympho, Richard Jeanty $14.95 Available
43. Meeting Ms. Right's Whip Appeal, Richard Jeanty $14.95 Available
44. Me and Mrs. Jones, K.M Thompson $14.95 Available
45. Chasin' Satisfaction, W.S Burkett $14.95 Available
46. Extreme Circumstances, Cereka Cook $14.95 Available
47. The Most Dangerous Gang In America, R. Jeanty $15.00 Available
48. Sexual Exploits of a Nympho II, Richard Jeanty $15.00 Available
49. Sexual Jeopardy, Richard Jeanty $14.95 Available
50. Too Many Secrets, Too Many Lies, Sonya Sparks $15.00 Available
51. Stick And Move, Shawn Black $15.00 Available
52. Evil Side Of Money, Jeff Robertson $15.00 Available
53. Evil Side Of Money II, Jeff Robertson $15.00 Available
54. Evil Side Of Money III, Jeff Robertson $15.00 Available
55. Flippin' The Game, Alethea and M. Ramzee, $15.00 Available
56. Flippin' The Game II, Alethea and M. Ramzee, $15.00 Available
57. Cater To Her, W.S Burkett $15.00 Available
58. Blood of My Brother I, Zoe & Yusuf Woods $15.00 Available
59. Blood of my Brother II, Zoe & Ysuf Woods $15.00 Available
60. Hoodfellas, Richard Jeanty $15.00 available
61. Hoodfellas II, Richard Jeanty, $15.00 03/30/2010
62. The Bedroom Bandit, Richard Jeanty $15.00 Available
63. Mr. Erotica, Richard Jeanty, $15.00, Sept 2010
64. Stick N Move II, Shawn Black $15.00 Available
65. Stick N Move III, Shawn Black $15.00 Available
66. Miami Noire, W.S. Burkett $15.00 Available
67. Insanely In Love, Cereka Cook $15.00 Available
68. Blood of My Brother III, Zoe & Yusuf Woods Available
69. Mr. Erotica
70. My Partner's Wife
71. Deceived 1/15/2011
72. Going All Out 2/15/2011

Name_____
Address_____
City_____State_____Zip Code_____

Please send the novels that I have circled above.
Shipping and Handling: Free
Total Number of Books_____Total Amount Due_____
        Buy 3 books and get 1 free. This offer is subject to change without notice.
Send institution check or money order (no cash or CODs) to:
RJ Publications
PO Box 300771
Jamaica, NY 11434
For more information please call 718-471-2926, or visit www.rjpublications.com
Please allow 2-3 weeks for delivery.